THE HOLE IN THE WORLD

THE HOLE IN THE WORLD

BY BRANDANN R. HILL-MANN

atmosphere press

Published by Atmosphere Press

Cover design by Dominique Wesson
dominiquewessonartblog.tumblr.com

10 9 8 7 6 5 4 3 2 1

The Hole in the World
2019, Brandann R. Hill-Mann

atmospherepress.com

For Cara

This could not exist without you.

CHAPTER ONE

Kahrin

There was something so invigorating about the burn of cold, January air being drawn through a hot trachea. It wasn't take-advantage-of-the-tilt-steering-car-sex good, but it was pretty damned close, in Kahrin's opinion. Every breath was a clarifying, almost painful reminder of being alive. The way her nose froze shut for just a second if she sniffled too hard, and the trail of steam that followed her every exhale. The juxtaposition of hot and cold native to winter training was the only good thing about having to actually train through the winter.

The rhythmic thuds of her footfalls picked up in tempo as she came out of the far curve, using the momentum to quicken to a sprint as she opened her stride into the straightaway. Arms pumping back and forth clear of her sides. Chin jutting forward as she leaned into the stride. Slush kicked up by her spikes throwing a rooster tail up the back of her sweater. As much as she hated the wet and the cold, being alone with just her body, uninhibited by decorum or other people around her, was what being alive was meant for. Moving.

She slowed through the next curve, long, lazy steps to the next straightaway, where she turned on the balls of her feet, jogging backward as she passed by the home bleachers. At the very bottom, arms draped through the rail, face obscured by a massive, fluffy scarf of orange and powder blue made by her mother, was her best friend, and biggest fan.

"You know," she called up as she trotted toward Innes, "I bet you'd be less cold with like, a hat. Or a hood. Ma says you lose all your body heat through your head."

"How dare you!" he grumbled, affectionate teasing in his big, bistre eyes, his low voice muffled from the scarf. "A hat? On this head of hair?"

"The horrors." She hopped up, planting her heels on the front of the stands and clinging to the rail with her knit-gloved hands to keep her balance. Even then, the soft scrape of her spikes on the concrete could be heard as she fidgeted. "You might have to settle for being just regular handsome, instead of ruggedly so." She reached up, hand positioned to tousle his prematurely greying hair, muted silver in the overcast afternoon light. As she predicted he leaned back out of her reach as she did.

"You're trying to butter me up," he accused. His grin told her it was working.

Kahrin scoffed, pretending to be scandalized. "I am offended, Pretty Mouth."

"You can be offended, but save us all time and tell me what you want." His brow creased as he stood, his full foot of height over her possibly meant to make him appear imposing.

It didn't work. "A ride home. Which you were going to give me anyhow, because you're my best friend, and you love me."

"How else were you going to get home?" he asked, lifting a brow. No seventeen-almost-eighteen year-old boy had any right having brows naturally arched so perfectly.

Kahrin dropped her head back, the end of her dark braid swinging loose at her backside. "Ugh. Why do you make me ask every day? You know you're going to drive me home." She didn't have a license. It was too far to walk. Even too far to run.

"Maybe I like hearing you beg." He leaned forward and bumped his nose against hers.

She rolled her eyes, though the smile that curved her lips and eventually showed her teeth belied her amusement. "Your sick pleasure over my discomfort is not attractive."

"Liar."

"Do hapless maidens like that about you?" she asked as she dropped back to the track, her spikes clacking into the rubbery surface.

Ignoring her goading, Innes picked up his nerd-sized knapsack and slung it over his shoulder on one strap. "Are you finished?"

She hopped up and down, shaking out her legs in her powder-blue running tights. "Yeah, I'll stretch in the car."

"I can wait while you stretch here," he said, hopefully.

Intentionally oblivious to the hint of plea, Kahrin reached under the rail and dragged her ruck from under the bench. "The track's wet, the concrete is too cold. My butt will cramp." She made a vague gesture to her rear. "Do you want my butt to cramp? Because that's how we get butt cramps."

Innes shook his head, smartly resigning himself that it was easier to give in than argue further, and hopped over the rail to the ground. He jerked his chin toward the parking lot, indicating they should get going. Middle of the

5

winter, the sun was already setting.

She fell into step beside him, taking longer ones as he shortened his. "Are you going to make me ask you to pick me up for the party, too?"

He chuckled as he pushed the gate to the track open for them to pass through. "What are you going to do next year when I'm not here to taxi you around?"

Kahrin pressed her lips together, not wanting to get into this again. Yes, Innes was going to leave this town. As soon as he could, he'd go anywhere but here to get out of his brother's house. She couldn't blame him, really. She would hate sharing a bedroom with her nephew, and on bunk beds no less. She accepted his leaving as readily as she accepted that she was likely not getting past the welcome sign of this nowhere pit stop. Did he need to remind her every day?

"That's future Kahrin's problem," she declared, the clack of her spikes on the sidewalk growing louder as she became more agitated. "Present Kahrin is worried about how to get to her joint birthday party with her best friend."

The side of his mouth hooked upward as he opened the door of his little sedan for her. "I have a change of clothes in my bag. I'll shower and change at yours." He pecked her cheek and waited as she slung her bag into the back seat before flopping into the passenger seat.

"You were planning to drive me, the whole time."

"Maybe." He smirked, patting the hood as he rounded the front of the car and slid into the driver's seat. "Or, I have to be prepared for your demanding and changing whims at all times."

"Har, har."

Kahrin kicked her spikes off as he turned them out of

the lot, winding through the neighborhood surrounding their school. She stretched out her arms, first, taking advantage of his attention being focused on the road to ruffle his hair anyhow. Sometimes it was fun just to wind him up and see how much he'd put up with before he retaliated. It was no fun when he didn't give her the satisfaction of a rise.

Kahrin propped both heels up on the dashboard, reaching forward to grab her feet, feeling the stretch in her hamstrings. She laid her head against her knees, turning to watch him drive, noticing the very slight whitening of his knuckles. Wow, he was really fighting hard.

She rotated her ankles, then sat back in her seat, leaving her feet where they were.

"If we get into a crash, your shinbones are going to impale you." He glanced at her, briefly, as he turned onto tree-lined back road that led out of town proper, to the farms.

"I have faith in your driving." Which wasn't the point, and she stared at him as the tendon tightened in his jaw. "Is something wrong?"

"Kahrin." The warning in his voice brought an amusement to it.

"What? As your oldest and dearest friend, your well being matters to me. If there's anything I can do, you know you need only . . . ask." How the ground did not swallow them up as she beamed up at him, the picture of innocence, not even the greatest scientists could say.

"Kahrin," he started slowly, emphasizing every syllable, "would you mind taking your feet off the dash?"

She lifted her brows, expectantly.

"Please," he added grudgingly.

7

"Oh! I didn't realize." One after the other, she lowered her feet to the floor of the car, then tucked them up under her. He sighed, but she could still see the glint in his eye.

She fiddled with the radio—a decade of friendship had earned her that right—and settled on what her ma called Classic Rock but the DJs decided was Oldies a few years ago. They had a good twenty minutes left of the ride, and the sun was setting in front of them. Even Kahrin knew not to mess with his concentration right now, the glare on the wet road making vision a challenge, even with his aviators on. The last thing they needed was to run off the road and get stuck in a ditch in the five-mile stretch with no cell service. Her eyes flicked to him, then back to the road, then back to him again. Apparently her two miles of circuits hadn't burned everything out of her.

"Ma and Dad had to go into town for a co-op meeting. There was some fuss about someone's rooster. Who knows when they're going to be home."

His smile climbed a little higher. "You're ridiculous."

"What? I'm just saying. It's Friday. My brothers are probably already out doing whatever brother things they do." There was no end to the list of possibilities of what Alec and Brecken were up to. Tipping cows was not beyond the list of possibilities. More likely, Alec convincing Brecken that cows could be tipped, and their eldest determined to prove he could do it.

"Let me guess. You want to," he added a meaningful pause, "study? Biology? You need a math tutor?" He knew very well what she was hinting at. Today's game was apparently using your words.

"Fractions. I was hoping you could help me visualize one of your three thirds?" She shrugged at the snort he let, unsure if she saw his cheeks redden or not. It was difficult to tell in this light. "Look, I never would have known how great sex is if you hadn't introduced me to it. I was a pure and hapless maiden before you got me alone."

Another snort, this one accompanied by a clearing of his throat. "How are you not tired out? I'm exhausted just from watching you run."

She twisted sideways in the seat, wiggling around to gain slack on the seatbelt. "You're the smart one. Ever hear of endorphins?" She leaned up, nuzzling into his neck, forgetting her earlier vow not to be distracting.

"Kahrin," he laughed, squirming. "You're not wearing your belt right." He paused, turning his head to look at her. "You can wait until your house. At least the driveway. Hm?"

Oh, a 'hm?' was it? She beamed, wiggling around in her seat again to right herself. "As you wish."

Barely had she settled forward-facing again than the car skidded on a patch of ice. With deft practice—not that they would ever be reckless on the back roads—Innes turned the wheel against the sliding one way and then the other. The car lurched as he took his foot from the accelerator. Kahrin gripped the shoulder strap of the seatbelt, letting out a little shriek that she quickly muffled, not wanting to make the situation worse.

The car skidded off the asphalt, scraping a bank of snow before he veered back onto the road once more. He let a nervous laugh. "That was close—"

"Innes! Look out!" Kahrin shouted, pointing at the dim figure of a small person running into the street. The girl, hair erratic, stopped in the lane and stared at them, like a deer in headlights.

"Shit!" He stamped his foot on the brakes, cranking the wheel to one side to avoid hitting the slight young woman, her hands throwing out in front of her.

The car spun, a bright flash whirling about them, then barreled off the road, sliding through the slippery snow, and whacking into the trunk of a tree on the passenger side. Kahrin's head bounced off the glass, and she only managed a glance to make sure Innes wasn't dead before she blacked out.

Innes

Innes stared ahead, unfocused. Not entirely certain what had just happened. The strap of his seatbelt held him to the seat, far more snug than felt comfortable. He breathed in shorts gasps, mostly to make sure he still could.

"Are you okay?" He turned to look at Kahrin, blinking away the dazzle from his eyes, feeling his stomach turned to stone. She was against the window, her neck at a weird angle over her seatbelt strap. "No, no, no," he stammered over and over, struggling to unbuckle the restricting the seatbelt. "Kahrin?"

She didn't move, and he pulled his glove off, reaching to check her pulse right away, his shaking, pale fingers against her brown skin. Relieved by the faint thrum, he pushed his mind to his first-aid knowledge. He rattled through the steps because the steps would keep him calm when he certainly did not want to be calm. He looked up and down the road, not seeing any vehicles coming. He asked if she was okay, even knowing she would not answer. He removed his aviators and held them in front of her face, letting a groan of relief when her breath fogged the mirrored lenses. He blinked rapidly, clearing the water from his vision and reached across her to lie the seat back, just enough to keep her head elevated.

"Help!" A high shriek preceded the smacking of hands on his driver's side window, making him jump. In faint twilight Innes could make out the features of the frightened young woman, her eyes wild and hair fanned out in frizzy waves. "They're going to catch me. Please."

The terror in her voice gripped his chest. He checked for Kahrin's pulse one more time before leaving a quick kiss on her brow. "I'll be right back. Stay here." Where was she going to go? Knowing her, he wasn't taking any chances. Part of him hoped she'd sit up and tell him that he was not her supervisor and she'd go anywhere she chose. She didn't, and Innes had to hope for the best.

He tumbled out of the car, boots hitting the snow as he put his weight onto unsteady legs. He wobbled, grasping at the roof of the car with one hand to catch his balance. "Who's after you?"

The young woman shook her head, her thin, shaking hands digging into her messy hair and let out a wail so heartbreaking it physically hurt Innes' chest. "I don't know! I just know someone is." Instinctively, he moved to comfort her with a hand on her arm, and she shrank away from him, as if shoved by some invisible force. "Don't touch me!"

He held his hands up, palm out, and backed until he felt his shoulder blades hit the frame of the car door. As soon as she said it, he knew, somehow, that he shouldn't have tried it in the first place. "It's okay. I won't touch you." He met her eyes, impossibly colorless in the low light and felt his chest squeeze, the breath leave his lungs, knowing she would hold him to that promise. "I can help you," he assured her, unsure if he could, but having no doubt that he would go to the ends of the Earth to try.

Stooping down, Innes fumbled around in first his coat pockets and then the console of the car for his phone and turned on the flashlight. The woman backed into the road, wailing as if her life was ending. If asked, he'd have sworn to it as fact that she was in great peril. He had no signal bars on his screen. Just as he'd feared, they were in the brief dead zone between town and the Quirke farm.

"Are you okay? Can you walk?" he asked, trying to keep his voice as gentle as possible. Not an easy feat, his heart racing away and the ever-growing panic shaking his words.

The girl looked at him, her face pinched. She tugged at her hair, her filthy sweater, and her leggings. She scratched fingers over herself, squirming as if they were foreign sensations on her skin. "Of course I can walk!" she snapped. She rolled her shoulders back, standing tall with challenge. Her neck was almost too long, her head almost too big, and her eyes almost too far apart, all of it adding up to a rather devastating effect of beauty which Innes was sure he would not soon forget.

He nodded once, gesturing her to follow. She took three steps and staggered forward as if she'd just learned to walk. He rushed to catch her, and she rolled her weight away from him, falling to the snowy ground. "I said don't touch me!" Her eyes widened again in a blazing panic, nostrils flaring as she snorted audibly. She rolled to her feet with all the grace of a newborn foal.

"Okay. You might be hurt. I need you to stay here. My friend is hurt, and I don't want to leave her alone." He pulled the driver's side door open for her, watching helplessly as she struggled to pull herself up onto the seat. "I know you're scared, but I have to go find a cell signal." Explaining his every thought kept him moving forward, kept his thoughts logical. He was fine. Kahrin was probably fine, though being unconscious and the absence of that rich color to her brown face wasn't promising. The young woman in front of him was hopefully fine, as well.

The young woman turned to look at Kahrin's form, reaching a hand out toward her with odd concentration, then pulling it back, startled. "Why?" She shook her head, perplexed as she looked down at her hand, and tears welled up in her again, a sob choking her throat.

He didn't have time to calm her, no matter how much his heart yearned to do so. His instinct was to help her, at any cost, but the time it took wouldn't get his best friend the help she needed. It wouldn't help any of them. "Keep her safe," he instructed, knowing it was foolish. They were both hurt. They couldn't do anything for one another. Which meant he had to hurry. Remembering the cold, he took off his parka and draped it over her lap. "I promise I'll be right back. Keep the car running to stay warm."

She nodded, his words making no sense to her, judging by her blank expression.

He had no way of knowing which direction was closer to a signal. Innes took a deep breath, closed his eyes, and waited for a direction to pull him. He turned, the thudding crunch of his boots on the snow quickening as his long strides worked up to a run.

CHAPTER TWO

Kahrin

"Where's Innes?"

Kahrin's eyes opened to harsh fluorescent lights and the stuffy antiseptic smell of a hospital room. Leads and wires connected her to a series of annoyingly beeping machines and, wow, did her head hurt. Someone was talking to her, and honestly she didn't care what they were saying because not one word of it answered her very important question of *where is Innes?* She shifted to sit up, feeling a wash of dizziness threaten to knock her over, and a roil of nausea that must have been clear on her face, as a small basin was quickly brought to her.

"Easy. Try to keep still." Any other time, the nurse hovering over her to get her to sit still might have deserved a bright smile, or made her blush. He had a nice face and a voice so low that she might have found pleasing. Since he was getting in her way, however, he instantly went from "cute" to "obstacle to be defeated."

"Screw being still!" She jerked her arm away from him while he tried to attach a blood pressure cuff to her and waved a hand to keep the thermometer at bay. "Where. Is. Innes?"

He looked at her, befuddled. "Your friend? The driver?"

"No, Innes, the Queen of Canada," she snapped. "Yes,

the driver. My best friend. Where is he?" The longer she lay there, the longer her questions went unanswered—no matter that it was only a matter of minutes—the more panic rose in her voice.

"You hit your head, miss, so I need—"

"No shit, I hit my head!" she shrieked this time. "I need to know if he's okay!"

Possibly in response to her theatrics, the doctor came in then, and Kahrin was forced to endure his little pen light in her eyes. A few bumps and prods as he checked, presumably, to make sure she hadn't sloshed some brain out of her head in. . . . She rumpled her face up in thought. How did she hit her head?

"He's with your other friend," the nurse explained, which did not mollify Kahrin at all. That made no sense and didn't answer her question remotely.

"We don't have other friends." She scrabbled at the pressure cuff, pulling the Velcro free. "No one likes us."

That was a slight exaggeration, but she couldn't be bothered with details right now, as the nurse tried, and received some bony elbows for his efforts, to keep her in the bed. Of course they had other friends. People without friends did not have birthday parties thrown for them. Who in the world was Innes fussing with that he wasn't right next to her so she could make sure that he was okay? That was abominably rude of him.

Intent on her goal, Kahrin paid no attention to the nurse trying to get her back into bed or the doctor insisting she rest. After shrieking at them about why she couldn't remember what happened, the nurse relented and agreed to take her to find Innes, if she consented to riding in a wheelchair.

She grunted her compliance without admitting that she thought she might fall and smack her head again if she walked. She grudgingly accepted the help out of the bed and appreciated his assistance in a very nonverbal way. Exceptionally polite, in her opinion, considering she didn't know where Innes was.

Innes was, of course, pacing. Parka and scarf discarded in a waiting-room chair and hands jammed in his sweater pocket, agitation foremost in his actions. Back and forth, back and forth.

"Innes!" she called. She threw her hands up in unspoken demand that he explain himself.

He looked toward her, relief morphing his expression. "Kahrin. You're awake." He was by her side in just a few long-legged steps. The nurse surrendered custody of the wheelchair to Innes, as if he were given the option by either of them.

"Yeah. And you weren't there. You're okay? They wouldn't tell me where you were, or if you were okay. I was afraid you were dead and they were just trying to do that thing where they keep me ignorant to keep me calm."

"I'm fine." The affection was there, but the tension overwhelmed it, his brow tightening at the way her words slurred despite her efforts to enunciate. "Your parents are on their way, I think. Brecken said he was going to town to find them." Of course. Because her parents would have shut their phone off for their meeting. "How are you feeling?"

"Sick," she said honestly before waving it off. "What happened?"

Naturally, he asked twice more before accepting her answer as truth. He relayed the story, some of the pieces

16

coming back to her, others staying just out of reach no matter how hard she tried to grasp it. His car was salvageable, though the passenger door wasn't opening, which Kahrin reassured him would not prevent her from riding in his car, and not to worry. Miraculously, he was unharmed, apart from being shaken up from nearly hitting a person. And that pesky bit where she'd been knocked unconscious. He fussed over her too much. Honestly. He couldn't un-bruise her brain.

The conversation lasted long enough to bring them to where they stood now, just outside the door of the girl they'd barely avoided. "She has no idea who she is. None. They had to sedate her to even get her to stay in bed because she wouldn't let anyone touch her." Kahrin lifted her brow, looking at Innes with a little suspicion, that hint of wonder in his voice as he watched the girl sleep from their vantage point in the hallway. Pulling her lips to the side in a pucker, Kahrin studied her from the doorway. She was pretty. More than pretty. The kind of pretty that could make your heart stop if she caught you by surprise. By, just for one example, running out in front of your car. Even sleeping, even with her fluffy blonde hair in disarray, she was indeed lovely. Despite the little pang of jealousy in Kahrin's stomach, which was already pissed off from the nausea, she knew it wasn't any sort of crush or lust in his voice. Just awe.

"A frantic amnesiac running in front of your car and nearly killing us?" Under normal circumstances, she might have accepted that alone as his interest. Which would have only lasted so long as there was doubt to her being okay, which she had to concede was fair as he was the one who almost hit her. "Okay, Pretty Mouth, out with it."

"Out with what?" Oh, he was too damned good at feigning innocence. Hand him his BAFTA already. She gave him a look, chastisement and annoyance mixed with the tired way her eyes didn't want to stay focused. "Fine. Hold on."

He wheeled the chair around, pushing her back down the hall until they reached her room. Blissfully empty of any bothersome medical professionals. She grew up on a farm. They could bring a pail of dirt and she could just rub some on and walk out. "I think she actually saved us."

"What?" Kahrin dropped her head back with a groan, immediately followed by a hiss of pain as this exceeded even her odd thrill for it. "I don't feel very saved." She actually felt like her brain was ready to evacuate through her ear or nose, forcibly if necessary. She clutched her head to stop the room spinning.

"Do you remember the flash of light?"

"You mean the headlights reflecting off of everything?" It was all kind of a blur. "Sure."

"No," he insisted. Turning her to face her bed, he rested on the edge of it. "I think that was her."

Oh, no. "What do you mean, 'that was her'?"

She knew perfectly well what was coming, even before he whispered the answer. "Magic."

She did her best to just smile. If you loved Innes, you loved this about him. Loved the way he believed faeries had crept into his room in the 'tween hours as a child. She'd never seen the faeries, of course. There was a certain charm to how ardently he believed in fantasy. His parents had been alive then. "You read too much."

"You don't read at all," he pointed out. Touché! "That doesn't mean I'm not right."

"I have you to read to me, but that's not the point. We almost hit a person. I whacked my head, which hopefully isn't going to change much," she really wanted him to laugh so she felt better, "and now we'll have to get your car fixed so I don't have to take a bus. I might have to touch someone on a bus. There's nothing magic about that."

"How do you explain that I'm completely unscathed?" he enquired.

As usual, his stupid earnestness over this wore her down. "Wearing your seatbelt properly? The impact being on my side? Your head being harder than mine? Innes, magic is not the most obvious answer here." She pinched at the bridge of her nose. As much as their little chats about the impossible were fun, she was not well, and that sort of sucked the joy out of everything.

"Okay. Come on. Into bed with you."

"I'm fine."

He didn't even need to say anything. That line of his lips and the little flutter in the muscle of his cheek told her he not only disagreed, but knew she was lying. Truth was a cardinal rule between them, never to be broken.

"Okay. Whatever." She let him help her out of the chair and up into the bed, only because the bed wouldn't stay still long enough for her to aim appropriately.

He kicked his shoes off and climbed in next to her. Even were she in a mood to pretend she didn't want any of that cuddly *soft shit* crap, and she was not, he wasn't having it. Before she could think to feign protest, he curled around her. "How are you, really?"

"I don't think we're going to make that party." She snorted a soft laugh, regretting it as lightning arced through her head.

Which was fine, since he took over the soft laughter for them both. "You'll make it up to me. I'll add it to the tally."

"I thought we weren't keeping track of points?" She didn't even know numbers that high.

"You agreed to that, not me," he teased. He cradled her carefully, which made her want to sleep. He sensed it, she could tell, so he continued talking. "There's something about her. She's special."

"Then maybe you should be sitting in her room, waiting to get her number?" Kahrin huffed, petulant despite herself. "Or, her name."

He laughed. "Someone's jealous."

"Am not. Shut up."

He poked her gently in the ribs, which would have tickled any other time. "It's not like that. She's . . . pure."

"What is that supposed to mean?" she demanded. No, they weren't *like that* even though they were *like that*. They had no claim over one another. But if he was going to imply that she was dirty or damaged, she'd find the strength and focus to punch him.

He leveled her a look. "Don't do that," he rebuked gently. "I don't think she's human, Kahrin."

"Oh, my God." Half laugh, half groan, all regret. Again. "Don't say what I think you're going to say." This always happened, whatever book they read (okay, okay, he read, she listened) always started affecting his ideas about everything. She was too pretty to be a faery. They were landlocked, which cut out selkies and mermaids.

"I think she's a unicorn."

"Innes." Oh, she was going to write a strongly worded letter to Peter Beagle.

"What? I do!" Obviously. He didn't say things he didn't

mean. "She wouldn't let the paramedics or police touch her. They didn't even try. There's just something about her. We need to keep her safe."

She knew she was losing this argument that was definitely not an argument before she even asked her questions, sure that he'd have an answer to each and every one. "Then why did they bring her here, and not to a vet clinic? Oh, I know! Because she's a girl, just like me!" Except apparently not *just like her*, as she was pure and needed their protection.

"Because someone has turned her into a human," he said with the sort of conviction that brooked no argument. "So she won't remember who she is."

"Who would do that?"

Oh, he had an answer for this, too. "Probably an evil wizard." How did he do that? Say those words, in that order, and not crack up laughing. Except, it was one of her favorite things about him. Despite how studied and smart he was, he still believed in the magic of fairy tales, right down to the part where he'd play hero to a hapless maiden. And she'd support him if it made him happy. That's what best friends do.

Kahrin was spared having to concede the discussion by the return of the nurse, making it clear that her bed was made for one occupant, and one only. Innes obeyed without argument, which he left to Kahrin. Unfortunately, she had little argument left in her. Once the nurse was gone, he was right back up next to her, determined to keep her awake until her parents arrived. Then, Ma Quirke would take care of that, fussing over both of them. Loudly.

Innes

Kahrin's face poked out the back window of the farm truck to make sure Innes was in fact turning his poor car into the drive behind them. He pulled up to his spot behind the smaller goat pen where the grass was worn in exactly the track of his little sedan. Pickle, the Quirkes' pit bull, barreled out of the farmhouse, all solid muscle and stubbed tail with a blue-merle coat. He proceeded to jump up on everyone in turn to express just how happy he was to not have been abandoned.

Knowing she was still wobbly, Innes stepped between Kahrin and the dog, more than happy to let him stand up on his hind legs, resting his paws against his chest. Innes took the time to fuss him sufficiently so when he gestured Kahrin over to pet him, he didn't jump on her. She smiled, more than a little dazed, in gratitude.

Grainne Quirke ushered them into the house with a click of her tongue, like she was herding the hens back into the coop. She tutted and disappeared into the kitchen as soon as she had her house shoes on. "Innes, did you eat anything this week? You're too thin!"

"Yes ma'am," he answered dutifully. "They do feed me at home." He looked to Kahrin, helplessly. What was she going to do? Sometimes he thought Kahrin got a sick sort of pleasure at how her parents treated him.

As if she hadn't heard him at all, Ma Quirke called from the kitchen. "I think I have some of that roast you liked still in the fridge."

"Really, ma'am, you don't need to–" Iskandar cut him off with a nearly imperceptible shake of his head, arms crossed over his chest. Innes closed his mouth immediately, not wanting to cross the man. He never felt unwelcome in the Quirke home, but wasn't so foolish as to miss the very still and quiet way Da Quirke studied him. His eyes and skin were dark, his hair cut short and clean where the tattoos on his face disappeared into the hairline. Before Innes could protest further, the sound of the microwave beeps rang out.

"I wish it wasn't so late, so I could warm it in the oven. The microwave makes the meat so chewy." Her voice, rich and strong, carried into the dining room as she shuffled about her domain. "Innes, didn't you like that pie we had the other night?" He heard the pie plate clatter on the counter.

"I don't need pie, too, ma'am."

"You're getting pie, son. Don't be rude." Innes straightened his posture before Da Quirke was finished talking. Kahrin inherited much of the man's looks, though her skin and eyes were notably lighter, and used that same glare to similar, withering effect.

"Yes, sir." He shrugged out of his parka and took Kahrin's as well to hang in the mudroom.

"I'm going to shower," she announced.

"You're going to sit down and eat, is what you're going to do," Ma chirruped. "You'll at least have pie, so Innes doesn't have to eat alone."

Kahrin rolled her eyes, and Innes cringed at the way it made her wince. "He's been eating unattended for years, Ma. He even gets some of it in his mouth." Was that really necessary? Concussion or no, she didn't have to slight him so! Innes took his usual seat on the bench at the large farm table, and Kahrin settled beside him. "I'm covered in hospital goo and sweat." She was definitely grouchier than usual, not that he dared say such a thing. Pickle darted under the table and rested his nose on her knee, whimpering softly.

Whether they wanted it or not, dinner was presented, and Ma tried to keep chatter going as if nothing at all was wrong. No, she didn't blame Innes for the accident. No, Kahrin would be just fine. No, he was not driving home this late after everything that happened in that car.

"I'll pull out the trundle," Kahrin announced.

Da replied with a disapproving grunt that shot Innes' back rod straight. A real disapproval that was a little too knowing for his taste. Kahrin looked sideways at her Da, he looked level at her, and Innes knew beyond any doubt that Da *knew*. His face went hot, and he ducked it, trying to hide it between bites of roast.

"Oh, let it go," Ma rebuked Da gently. "Both boys are home, and you are not going to make him sleep on that lumpy mess we call a davenport."

"Innes has stayed the night before, Da." No! Kahrin, don't help! He didn't need her help!

Da grunted once more, the line of tattoo bisecting his eye adding to the appearance of sternness. "I know."

Da put the fear of God into him. It felt like the bite of roast in his mouth took forever to chew before he could swallow. Innes leaned over. "It's okay. I don't mind the couch."

"Davenport," Ma corrected him, even though it hadn't been unfolded for at least a decade. "And nonsense. Not when there's a perfectly good trundle upstairs in Kahrin's room."

Room was an exaggeration. It was more like a glorified closet off of Alec and Brecken's shared room. The A-frame ceiling slanted too low in most of it for Innes to stand up straight, but the Quirke house as a whole was not built for him. It was designed by and built for a family whose tallest member was five foot six inches. Innes had a foot, easy, over Kahrin's five foot one. Still. The room was hers, all to herself, and more private than the top bunk he had at home with Brodie. The only perk of being the only girl and youngest of three inside three years.

That didn't spare Innes the very stoic stare from Da Quirke. He had a good few inches over Kahrin's father, but the man didn't need height to be intimidating. His face, neck, and arms, bronzed darker from farm work, boasted a litany of tribal tattoos, and his quiet stillness unsettled most people. Except Kahrin. She wrapped him around any finger she chose with stunning ease.

Having eaten to Ma's satisfaction, they were dismissed. Innes carried Kahrin's ruck and his bag up the stairs, ducking through first Alec and Brecken's door, tolerating some light ribbing as they passed through the even smaller door to Kahrin's.

Kahrin turned the pin to wedge it shut and groaned as she kicked off anything that wasn't necessary. She flopped onto her bed, muffling a whimper as her head and neck bounced against the mattress. It didn't stop her from kicking her feet and sulking, "I need help getting my tights off."

"Yeah. About that." He hesitated in his spot, as if Da Quirke was going to barge through the door at any moment. "Does your dad *know*?"

"I guess?" she answered as she pushed down her running tights and wiggled as much as she could to get them to her knees. God forbid she could just put on or take off clothes. Why? When there was perfectly good bouncing and hopping and squirming to be done? "So?"

"So?" Innes barely touched the floor with his knees when he shot back to his feet. "Your dad hates me."

"Well, you did defile his hapless maiden of a daughter." She poked her tongue at him. Did she think this was funny? What if Da caught them and murdered him on the spot?

"Very funny," he muttered, drily. He relented, grasping ahold of her tights and peeling them the rest of the way off.

Innes busied himself with pulling out the trundle and clicked it into place while Kahrin fished her nightshirt from under her pillow. Once changed, the lights off, they snuggled down into their respective beds. Which lasted all of five minutes before Kahrin scooted down to the trundle and curled up against him. It didn't need to be said that she wasn't in a mood to fool around, which suited him just fine. That wasn't the point of their friendship of years, just a fun new aspect shared between them. She just wanted the comfort of him near her, and he was not inclined to argue as he wrapped himself around her. He wasn't going to deprive himself of cuddling if she was offering it without the pretense of disliking it. He kissed the top of her head.

He rubbed her back with a slow palm as he spoke. "I'm going to go back to the hospital tomorrow."

"What?" Kahrin shifted to see his face in the dark. No one had any business having eyes that large and pretty.

"To check on . . . well, you know. Her." He went still, waiting for her reaction.

"She's not your responsibility. Even the police said so."

"I know," he noted. Slowly so as not to jostle her, he sat up. "But I don't think she has anyone. I think she does need us."

"Us?" Surely she didn't expect to be excluded from this.

She couldn't complain about it, not after the many times he'd engaged in her shenanigans over the years.

He knew it, and she did too. "Well, I know you've basically peed on me now, so I figured you'd want to go and make sure nothing untoward happens." Ouch! There was no way he deserved the heel he took to his shin. "As if I'd even be worthy to touch an immortal being. No. It hurts my heart to even think of it." He was quiet a moment. "Kahrin, I think we're meant to protect her."

"You don't even know her," she objected. "Or her name. The beginning and end of your relationship is you not hitting her with your car." She huffed, wrapping an arm around him and making that sound they both knew meant she was going to give in. Oh, she thought his suspicions were silly, but she also knew it mattered to him. If it mattered to him, it mattered to her. That was just the way their bizarre little friendship worked. "Fine. After breakfast. Then you owe me one."

His mouth hooked up on one side as he settled back down onto the trundle. "One what?"

Kahrin shrugged, her eyes closing. "Get creative. We're keeping points, remember?"

CHAPTER THREE

Kahrin

If Innes needed any proof that Kahrin's parents adored him, their insistence that he drive the farm truck to the hospital while Da gave his car 'a look' should have put that to rest. It should have. But that would also have required Da to not give him the stink eye all through breakfast. Had Kahrin not spent most of the morning in a fog of confusion, nauseated, and dazedly trying to answer such challenging questions like where she left her running clothes and if she wanted one or two chocolate chip pancakes, she might have mitigated the teasing a little. As it stood, she had to apologize for her lack of wit as Innes clutched the wheel of the truck, slowly acclimating to driving a much bigger vehicle.

"You're excused," he said, "this one time, but only because you have a note from your doctor." He gave her a strained half-grin, most of his focus needed for driving.

"How magnanimous of you." She let out a small chuckle. "Just know, I want to roll my eyes at you, but you're being spared by my raging headache."

"A favor for a favor. I'll keep that in mind."

They kept up enough banter to keep her awake for the rest of the drive, which left her with energy to tease him about parking as far away from the hospital as possible to avoid all the other cars.

Fortunately for them, Pretty Mouth wasn't just a clever moniker. That best friend of hers had a charm about him that she took for granted. Sporting an abashed smile, combined with a twinkle in his eyes, he talked their way into finding Jane Doe. Since Innes had been the one who nearly hit her, the nurses were quite understanding of the concern shining in his theatrically Jersey-cow-like eyes. Honestly, if medical school didn't work out for him, he could look into Broadway.

As a bonus, either out of genuine concern or just because he could, Innes also talked them into another wheelchair, which Kahrin only grudgingly allowed him to talk her into using. Because she wanted to, not because she was still dizzy or tired. Of course.

Since the night before, their would-be friend had calmed considerably. Sitting up in her bed, her pale-blonde hair fell in combed waves over her shoulders. She glanced at them, briefly, before turning her gaze back out the window. "I've already told the others that I don't remember anything." Her voice sounded far away, as if they were hearing her murmur from the end of a long hallway.

"Um," Innes started, and stopped. Oh, wonderful. Great time to get tongue tied. Kahrin gestured to him, urging him to keep going. "Do you remember us?"

"Yes."

Well, that settled that. She was effusive, too, so that was nice.

"I wanted to apologize." He paused, waiting for an acceptance that never came. "For almost hitting you." He stepped in, pushing Kahrin in the chair ahead of him.

"There's no need." She sounded sad. Very sad. As if lost,

which Kahrin supposed made sense, as she had no idea who she was. "I ran in front of you," the girl reminded them. She turned back, her very clear eyes, almost colorless staring through them. It unsettled Kahrin, to say the least.

It didn't seem to have that effect on Innes. He stepped around the wheelchair, approaching her as one might a spooked animal. "Do you remember anything? Like, how you wound up in the woods?"

"Why does everyone keep asking me that?" Her voice rose in pitch, panic forming a sharp edge. "I said no, I don't remember. I wish I remembered. I wish I remembered anything!" She turned away, throwing herself to her side and hiding her face.

Innes' face showed nothing but devastation. His hand clutched at his chest, like her grief physically pained him. The whole of it broke Kahrin's heart to see. What a group they were. A supposed unicorn crying, her best friend all but falling to pieces over it, which was making her want to cry. Wonderful.

"I'm sorry," Innes offered, and Kahrin snapped her head to look at him. Sorry for what? They hadn't done anything to apologize for! "I didn't mean to upset you. I– I'm here to help. We are."

"You? What can you do?" The girl turned to face them once more, pointing at Kahrin. Kahrin sat up in the chair. "She doesn't want to be here."

When Innes looked at her, he frowned. "Kahrin?"

She blinked, a barn cat holding perfectly still to avoid notice. It didn't work, and Innes raised a brow and repeated her name. "I just don't think we're the right people to help. What can we do? We're kids."

He threw his arms out to the side, shaking his head at

her in disbelief. As if she were the crazy one here. Did anyone remember that she had actual brain damage?

"She doesn't even know her name! What are we going to do? Take her home?" A spike of agitation rose in her, and she couldn't even explain it. She wasn't mad at him. Or at the girl or unicorn or whatever she was. Kahrin rubbed at her face with the heels of her hands. "I'm sorry. I am. I just, my head." Oh, this damned concussion. "I can't think straight."

The agitation melted away from Innes and he crouched in front of her, resting his hands on her knees and looking up to meet her eyes. "Are you okay?"

She shook her head. "I'm fine." She couldn't even think clearly enough to lie.

"Why don't you wait outside? I won't be long. I promise. Then we'll go home." His smile hooked upward on one side. "I mean, I have to get my car, right?"

Kahrin tried to glare, but it hurt, and she settled for a weak laugh. He leaned up so she could press her brow to his, breath to breath. "Okay."

"Let me help you." The girl turned her legs in front of her, stepping to the floor as light as a feather and approaching on soundless steps. Innes backed out of her way, quickly, some sort of invisible boundary pushing him back. She laid her hands on Kahrin's head and looked in her eyes. "It should have protected you, too." She tilted her head, the confusion in her voice enough to bring tears to Kahrin's eyes. That confusion only deepened as the girl narrowed her eyes, her concentration intent and focused. "It's not working. Why isn't it working?"

"What?" Kahrin looked from the girl in front of them to Innes and back again. "Why isn't what working?"

31

The girl stepped back, shaking her head as she buried it in her hands. "It should have worked! Why didn't it work?"

Kahrin wheeled the chair back, wanting to put as much space between herself and the girl who was steadily losing her chill.

"What did you do to me?" she shrieked at Kahrin. "What did you do to me?"

Innes stutter-stepped, first toward the girl, then back, caught between his natural inclination to offer comfort, and whatever it was about her that repelled him. "It's okay."

Throwing her hands up, placatingly, Kahrin said, "I'm going. I'm going." She turned, wheeling herself out of the room, and toward the waiting area. She could hear the girl screaming at Innes, begging him not to touch her and to take Kahrin away.

"I'm sorry about my sister," a low voice said. "She means no harm."

Kahrin looked up from where her head was rested on her hands, her eyes falling upon a tall, blond man. Taller than Innes, his eyes clear and blue, but not the pale blue of the girl in the room. His appearance was almost painfully tidy, except for his swoopy blond hair that curled at the ends. Creased dark trousers. A collared shirt under an expensive-looking sweater that didn't even have any of the little pills sweaters were notorious for.

"Your sister?" Kahrin thumbed over her shoulder. "You know her, then?"

"Her name is Yelena. We were separated a few days ago." He took a labored breath, winded as though he'd just climbed twenty flights of stairs. "Our mother recently passed."

"Oh, I'm sorry for your loss," Kahrin murmured. So, she had a name, and family. That was good news. Innes would be so relieved!

"Thank you," he said in a breathy whisper with a polite bow of his head. "I'm afraid she's not taken the news very well. Mother was sick for so long." He shook his head, extending a hand. Kahrin accepted it, surprised at how cold it was. That wasn't the most alarming part, though. When he stepped closer, she saw more clearly that his skin was sallow, giving him a very sickly pallor, despite having otherwise handsome features. "Pardon my manners. Evan. Evan Greves."

"Kahrin. Kahrin Quirke." She rubbed at her brow, realizing she'd been staring. "Sorry. I was in an accident."

"You were in the car?" He gestured toward the girl—Yelena's—room. Kahrin confirmed with a nod. "Well, this makes more sense, then."

"How so?" Kahrin craned her neck. Innes had calmed Yelena, from the sound of it. Or lack of sound, at any rate. Kahrin looked back to Evan.

Evan lowered his head to speak more quietly. "Our mother died of brain cancer. Yelena started having delusions that she could cure her. Laying her hands on her." Like she had Kahrin. "She blames herself."

Kahrin made a low humming sound. She couldn't imagine losing one of her parents. But if she did, she had the comfort of knowing there were people who would take care of her. It was good that Yelena had family.

"Your boyfriend seems quite taken with her."

"We're not. . . . I mean," she waved it off as she trailed away. That was none of his business, and she frowned.

"My mistake," he said with a tired smile, showing even teeth. "You look like you should have a beau."

A beau? Who said that anymore? Her cheeks reddened, undoing the frown without her permission.

"He thinks," she stopped herself, feigning forgetfulness of her train of thought, though it wasn't hard to do. That was also none of his business. She wasn't going to tell a stranger, even a very cute one who maybe just hit on her, that Innes thought his sister was a unicorn. It was one thing for her to think he was absurd; she'd earned that right over the years. But Evan Greves? No. He didn't get to judge her best friend for the things that made him happy. For holding onto something that gave him hope when life had dealt him such a crap hand: mother dying, sickly and horrid father eventually dying. No one would take the goodness that had survived in Innes Cameron while Kahrin breathed to protect it. "He was worried. Felt responsible."

"What a generous spirit, your friend." He stepped toward the room. "I'll have to remember to thank him. Were you terribly injured?"

Kahrin shook her head. "A skosh of concussion. Nothing important damaged," she added as a joke.

"I hope your recovery is swift, Kahrin." He smiled at her, ticking the charm up enough to make her cheeks pink. "I am glad to have met you." He walked slowly, taking a pause at the door to rest upon it, apparently winded once more. "Yelena."

"No!" Yelena screamed, jumping up from her chair. "No, no you leave me alone!"

Evan introduced himself to Innes, over the shrieking of his sister, clearly used to the scene of things. Innes shook his hand slowly, his eyes a little too intense to be happy at this turn of events. "Please forgive me, I think my sister's had enough excitement for one day."

"I'm not your sister!" she screamed. "Please! Innes! I don't know him. Don't leave us alone!"

"I am very sorry. My sister and I are both grateful to you for finding her, despite the potentially terrible circumstances. Quite a miracle no one was more hurt than they were." Evan smiled at Kahrin again as she wheeled herself back into the room. Yelena's cries pounded like railroad spikes through her temples.

Seeing the conflict on Innes' face, and not wanting to make a scene, she reached for his hand. "Can we go home, please? Let her family take care of her?"

Innes' attention snapped to Kahrin right away, fresh concern pinching his handsome face. Even with that touch of guilt twisting Innes' lips (or maybe because of it), Evan Greves had nothing on her best friend. He nodded, glancing back as Yelena cowered in a corner, weeping. "Yeah. Let's get you home. This can't be helping your head."

"It was nice to meet you both." Evan smiled at Kahrin, tiredly. "I hope to see you again, very soon." Kahrin ducked her head and looked up from under her lashes, oddly abashed.

It was Innes' turn to narrow his eyes. "Let's go then, hm?" Uh, oh. A 'hm'? He took the handles of the wheelchair and pushed her out of the room. They were halfway to the elevator when he leaned down and whispered, "I don't trust him."

So, that was a thing.

Innes

Pickle whined, following behind Kahrin, his nails clacking on the kitchen floor as he moved from one side of her to the other. Innes watched Kahrin open and close doors on the time-worn cabinets, marking each pass with a grunt of exasperation at apparent defeat. It didn't matter what she was looking for, because she'd forgotten what it was. She scrubbed at her eyes, and he knew she was unwilling to admit it.

"Let me make you a sandwich?" Innes leaned his back against the cabinets, arms crossed. He didn't like watching her drift about, lost in her own house, but he didn't think she would thank him for fussing over her.

He was right. "You're not my ma." Her mouth drew into a pucker as she peered into the refrigerator. He watched her choose and discard several items. She didn't want roast, which went in the sandwiches, so he dismissed the sandwich plan. He could tell by the way she winced away from the refrigerator light that her head still hurt. "Sorry." She shook her head with great caution. "That's not what. . . . I don't know." She spun a circle in front of herself with a single finger as if she was going to conjure the thought out of the air.

Innes frowned. Usually he could make sense of the twists and turns of her thoughts and logic, but even he was at a loss. "You could sit down." She could, but she wouldn't, he knew.

Not yet willing to give up, she moved to the sink, lifting a glass from the drying rack and taking it to the water dispenser, finding the bottle empty with a note on it. She stared at what Innes recognized as her mother's loopy cursive, the expression on her face growing more pinched the longer she looked.

"Come on," he said to her in a low tone of concern. With a gentle hand at her back, he guided her into a chair at the breakfast nook, which she took with no argument. Dutifully, Pickle took up a spot partially under her chair, resting his chin on her foot. When he'd been a puppy he would fit beneath it easily, so this was his best attempt at compromise. Not the only one to compromise, as Innes took the note from her, reading it with a chuckle. "It's your mam, asking me to change the bottle. I'll get your water."

A weak smile cornered her mouth upward. He took a kitchen towel from the sink, slinging it over his shoulder as he went out to the porch to retrieve a new bottle. For as much as Kahrin's father terrified him, Ma Quirke was indulgently affectionate, and part of that odd affection manifested in her leaving chores for him to do when he was around. She thought it made him feel more at home, and while he'd never say so out loud, it did. Of course, the Quirke farm felt more like home than Brodie's house or anywhere he'd lived with their father. Ma said it was a waste of all that excessive height of his not to use it for her benefit. In fact, were he honest, he enjoyed changing the bottle. As a bonus, because they stored the bottles on the porch, the water was just this side of freezing when he brought a full glass to Kahrin.

"I'm not helpless, you know." Her frustration quickly shifted into agitation as she took a long drink, chugging it too fast. She'd been still too long, he knew, and she missed her morning runs. The injury also likely meant she'd be benched from training until the neurologist cleared her. This idleness only added to something that was already eating at her, leaving her full of unspent energy, demonstrated through the telltale bobbing of one foot.

"No, but you do have a concussion. A serious one, Kahrin."

"I don't need you fussing over me." She slumped in her chair, crossing her arms tight over her chest and forcing him to bite the inside of his cheek to keep from laughing at the adorably familiar act. Pickle let out a soft snuffle-bark to acknowledge he was as aggrieved as she that they could not go running together. She resented being cosseted at the best of times, and this was far from the best of times. He also knew she'd tolerate it from him over anyone else, though she'd never admit it out loud. He didn't need her to.

Innes still sighed, a frown tightening his jaw. The worst of this was knowing that her misery was not, like so many other times they'd gotten up to antics, her own creation. A pang of guilt twisted his stomach. "I was driving the car when you got hurt."

"You didn't make some weird scared girl–"

"Unicorn." Maybe he could have let that one go. Force of habit with them.

"Right. Unicorn-girl," she snapped back. "You didn't make her run in front of us, whoever or whatever she is."

"It's not Yelena's fault, either!" he argued, his voice rising defensively even as he tried to keep it calm for her sake. "She was scared and confused."

Kahrin rubbed at her temple, then held the half-drunk glass to her forehead. "Can we just say no one is at fault and it's just a thing that happened?"

"Kahrin," he started, stepping closer, but she didn't give him a chance to finish.

"I'm the one who got hurt, okay?" She seemed to question the sense of yelling at him at the same time he did, judging by the scrunch to her pretty mismatched eyes. "If I don't want it to be a big deal, it shouldn't be!"

"That's not how–," he cut himself off and vented his frustration in a hard let-out of breath. Kahrin watched him, worry etched on her features. Even though she believed that it just proved how much they loved one another, he did not like fighting with her. He'd been cautious with his temper his whole life, at least until they'd met years ago. He didn't avoid rowing with her like he did others, which he had to admit was refreshing in some ways. That didn't mean it was any easier to endure. "You got lucky. If you hadn't, I—I can't think about it."

"I'm going to be fine, Pretty Mouth." Her silly little moniker for him brought a reluctant smile to her face. She looked up at him from under her lashes, her expression shifting with all the swiftness of a storm changing directions. "You can't break me that easily."

"Don't you dare," he said with a laugh.

"What?" she asked, the very picture of innocence. How lightning did not strike her for such audacity he would never know. "I don't know what you're thinking about. Here, alone, in a great big empty house."

Innes shook his head, affectionate exasperation on his face as he leaned down and caught her up in a brief kiss. Keeping up with her mood swings could really tire a man out. "You can't be bouncing around. Your doctor said no vigorous activity." He straightened himself up and brushed his hands as if he were ridding them of crumbs. "Now, let's try to remember what it was you wanted to eat."

The mention of food brought Pickle out from under Kahrin's chair, and he let a deep woof to let Innes know he approved of this idea. And one more woof in case anyone forgot he liked food, too.

The frown creased her brow again, her finger turning circles once more. He could tell it was right there in her mind. Likely she could even see it, but couldn't recall the words for it.

"Is it round?" he asked.

Kahrin blinked at him, not understanding that he'd drawn that conclusion from her hand gesture, then nodded. "I think so. It's round and the things are round."

"The things?" Frustration clear, he fought to make sure she didn't think it was directed at her with a brush of her cheekbone under his thumb. He wasn't used to not being able to predict her wants and needs. "What things? Bread things?" She shook her head. "Cookie things? Chocolate chips are round." She shook her head again and he rubbed a hand over his face. "Try to focus."

"I am!" She gripped her hands into fists and winced. "I am," she said again, quieter this time, looking up at him with regret in her expression. She drew her hand around in circles again, then started making crisscross patterns by winding her fingers together. "Ma makes it. The top is like this."

Innes rushed to the refrigerator, hope spurring his steps, and pulled out the pie plate that still had enough for two slices. "This?"

"Yes!" Even as excited as she was that they figured it out, she burst into tears, making his chest squeeze. "I'm sorry. This isn't your job, to take care of me like this. I'm practically an adult."

That made them both laugh, Kahrin despite her tears. "Well, that's terrifying," he ribbed gently as he set the pie plate on the table between them. He plucked two forks from the drawer before sitting beside her at the table. "I don't mind. You do the same for me. Remember when I had chicken pox?"

"Of course I do. Who still gets chicken pox?" People whose dickhead father didn't bother to keep up with their vaccinations, that's who. "I couldn't miss that chance to mock you for it." It helped keep the truth of it from weighing down upon him. "And it was lucky, besides. Who else would have kept me company after I separated my tailbone on the toboggan?"

"Lucky?" He popped a bite of pie into his mouth, rolling the familiar sweet-and-spicy combination of Ma Quirke's apple pie around on his tongue. The pie that had ruined all other apple pies for him. "Yeah, lucky you dragged your sick friend out sledding."

"Like you weren't dying to get out of the house." She took a giant bite, making Innes brace to do a Heimlich in case she'd overestimated her ability to swallow. He still had faith she could handle it, though. Call it a hunch. "I don't remember you suggesting we stay in."

"You've always been a terrible influence on me."

She pointed her fork at him. "Look who's talking."

Now it was Innes' turn to shrug in innocence. "I'm two-thirds innocent."

She nearly choked on her pie, coughing up a bit of crumbled crust. "Arguable!"

They ate in silence for a few minutes, Kahrin scarfing down as much of the filling as she could, and 'accidentally' dropping a hunk of Ma Quirke's handmade crust. So fortunate that Pickle was there to clean it up!

"Did you get Yelena's brother's name?" he asked.

Kahrin looked up at him, frowning for a few breaths

while she processed what he'd said. He could see the irritation ebb in once more as she tried to remember. Kahrin always joked that she wasn't a smart girl, which she believed made her less culpable for her poor impulse control. People expected less of pretty girls, she always argued, even if he vehemently disagreed. But she wasn't used to this. "He had some kind of, I don't know, emo boyband name. Egan. Alan." She paused. "Evan!" She said the last with wag of her fork. "Evan Greves. Why?"

"I want to check in with Yelena. Will you come with me? After school?"

The wrinkle of her brow assured him that was the last thing she wanted to do. Yelena was unwell, which was difficult on Kahrin's best days. He was so earnest in his concern, though, that she surrendered. Despite the little twinge of unwarranted jealousy—there was no breaking their friendship after all this time—that meant she had only one option.

"If it's that important to you, how could I say no?"

"Thanks." It wasn't just lip service. If it mattered to him, it mattered to her, and his thanks was an acknowledgment of that. Of the way she fiercely protected him and what was important to him. He scooped up the empty pie plate and forks, carrying them to the sink to wash. "But, first, how about a nap? Full belly, warm dog, best friend?"

Admittedly, he was tired, too, and he could see the idea appealed to her. It pushed away some of the lingering irritation the pie had not cleared out, and her pretty smile found its way back. She nodded as she waited for Innes to finish up his chore, then followed him to the living room, Pickle dutifully trotting behind, where the three of them pulled all the cushions from the davenport. They fashioned a nest with the pair of worn-out beanbag chairs and age-worn quilts. Kahrin snuggled into his side as he smoothed a hand over her hair and back, soothing her. She laid her head on his chest as she was wont to do and listened to his heart beneath her ear as she quickly fell asleep. He kissed the crown of her head, following soon after.

CHAPTER FOUR

Kahrin

Even pushed up on her toes, Kahrin could only manage to barely wrap her fingers over the top of the chain-link fence. It was still enough to hold her up as she watched the other runners with a longing so intense it bordered on devastation. It wasn't fair that the doctors and coaches wouldn't let her even walk on the track while the others ran. They could trust her not to push beyond what she could handle! Maybe. It wasn't like she'd try running with a concussion. Probably. Okay, fine, they were smart to forbid her going inside the fence, but that didn't change how unfair it was that she couldn't run.

The day was perfect for it. Sun peeked through the clouds, taking the nip out of the air but not making it too warm to breathe. That same sun had melted the snow from the rubber surface, leaving it damp, but not the sloshing mess that would send mud and water up her butt as she sprinted. Large, fluffy flakes of snow fluttered from the sky in loopy spirals, clinging to her eyelashes and dotting her hair with sparkling wisps.

Carbry was doing a long day, which they usually did together on Mondays. Five miles at an easy pace, throwing a little punk talk back and forth between them. They weren't always the nicest to one another, but it was nothing other than a little friendly competitiveness to make the miles go by. There was often a little flirting, too, but it started and ended with whose rear looked better in tights. He shook his head in her direction as he took the curve past her. A teasing rebuke for her slacking off. Her lewd gesture back at him wasn't the most mature response, but it felt good. That's all she wanted right now.

"Kahrin, right?"

She turned her head enough to see a figure coming up beside her, bundled in what looked like a very expensive peacoat with a cashmere scarf wound around his slim throat.

"Mm-hm." She blinked, trying not to look like she was struggling to remember the man's name. For crying out loud, she'd not met him long ago, how could she forget already?

"Evan," he reminded her. "Evan Greves." He added a lift to the end to reassure her it was fine if she didn't remember.

"Right." She nodded, releasing the fence and dropping flat onto her feet. She crossed her arms over her chest, tucking her knit-gloved hands under her arms. "Sorry. I'm not usually so . . ." she turned her hand over in front of her in loops.

He smiled, in an odd and refined way. Kind of like he'd spent time in front of the mirror learning how to pull that smile off to the best effect. Eyes crinkling and dimples making charming divots in his pale, flushed cheeks. "Stricken with concussion?"

She couldn't help her smile. "Yeah." She glanced over, noticing a cane in his hand, a rich wood polished to a glossy finish with a stone-cut hand rest. The way he leaned on it indicated it wasn't just for show, and she couldn't recall if he'd had it the other day. Of course, she couldn't recall what she'd eaten for dinner last night, either. "What happened?" she asked, realizing how rude that was only a moment later. She winced. "You don't have to answer that."

"This?" he asked, holding the cane up, the mildest of amusement warming his smile. "I'm anemic," he explained, patience uppermost in his tone. "Some days are better than others. Today is one of the others."

Kahrin frowned. That certainly explained the yellow tinge to him. "Should you be sitting?" she asked with new concern. She gestured with a nudge of her chin. "There's a bench over there."

"That would be lovely. Thank you." Such manners! He walked with very slow steps to the bench and very carefully used his cane to help him lower to sitting. He gestured an invitation to the space next to him. Kahrin chose to stand, leaning her weight against her butt, supported by the fence.

"Do you intend to stand out here every day, staring at them until you are better?" There was a hint of mirth his his voice.

"What?" It might have been her concussion, but she couldn't read him well enough to tell if he was flirting or simply being friendly. She also didn't know which she preferred. Hopefully it was chilly enough to make the pink on her cheeks unnoticeable. "No. No, I don't do that." She looked out towards the track once more, sighing theatrically, then back. "I'm waiting for my friend."

"Oh, that's right. Your friend." Evan snapped his fingers. "Inez?"

"Innes."

"Yes, that was it."

She tilted her head and lifted a brow as she caught her boot heel on the chain links. Kahrin couldn't tell whether he was messing with her. Again, she wasn't in the right state of mind to be the best judge, but she couldn't shake the feeling that he hadn't actually forgotten. "He drives me home." Which was the least accurate way of explaining their relationship.

"You spend a lot of time together?" He folded both hands over his cane in front of him.

She gave up the pretense of not being defensive. "He's my best friend. Since forever."

He lifted a hand, as if it took great effort, and even ducked his head, giving her a peek at the way his hair curled upward from under the back of his flat cap. "I meant no offense. A curiosity is all."

A curiosity? She crossed her arms again, bouncing one heel on the ground. All the charm she wasn't sure he was turning on her lost its effect, and she frowned. "You know. I should probably go find him. He probably got distracted talking to one of the teachers. Smart boys, right?"

"Please," Evan said, lifting a hand. "I was hoping, Kahrin, that you might consider helping me out with a problem." His voice pitched low and smooth, his pleasant face asking her not to go.

She narrowed her eyes, but curiosity bolted her in place. "What problem?"

"As you're aware, my sister is ill." Yeah, that was pretty easy to put together. "I have treatments for my condition a few days a week, but after what happened to you, I dislike leaving her alone." Kahrin lifted and dropped her hands, urging him to get on with it. "I was hoping, since you're not able to run, you might be willing to use that time to sit with her."

Sit with her? Like a child? Kahrin shook her head. "I shouldn't. My head's off."

"You would only need to keep her company," he assured her. "You seem very nice." Nice was such an innocuous word, but when he said it, her cheeks pinked while something flipped over in her belly. "And I think you would be a good presence for Yelena."

"Well." Now that she thought about it, Innes would actually like that. He'd been concerned about her since the accident. "I mean maybe, if Innes will come with me. Just in case."

"That's actually my concern. Your–" he paused, his brows lifting in lieu of finishing his thought.

"Friend," Kahrin supplied with a hint of agitation. Whatever he was hinting at, true or otherwise, was none of his business, and she wouldn't confirm or deny anything beyond their friendship. It wasn't fair to Innes. "Best friend."

"Your best friend," he repeated, some sort of amusement in his eyes that she wished she hated. "He tends to indulge my sister's delusions." Oh. "It's not good for her."

"He likes stories, is all." She looked up toward the entrance to the school, wondering what was keeping Innes, as a flare of protectiveness surged in her. "He would never hurt someone on purpose. He's the best person I know."

Evan lifted a hand in concession. "Like I said, I meant no offense. My first priority is my sister. I want her to get well, and I'm afraid I'm unable to do what needs to be done on my own. Would you help me, Kahrin?" He reached out to touch her arm, and even though she was pressed against the fence, she shrank back more.

"Why me? I don't know you." Kahrin gave him a nervous chuckle, and rubbed at her temple. She wound a stray lock of hair around a finger. "I'm a teenage girl, with brain damage. You're," she shrugged, "not." Her weight shifted from foot to foot.

He laughed, the sound rich and breathy from his obvious fatigue. "You are indeed a lovely young woman, but my interest in you is related solely to my sister." He covered his eyes with a gloved hand, still laughing. "Though, twenty-three is not so much older than you. Not in the big picture." Another weak chuckle. She was apparently killing with that assumption. Finally, he relented. "Alright. Bring your friend, if it makes you feel safer. Yelena needs a friend, and," he lowered his voice, "you don't believe their fantasies."

Abashed at her arrogance, she returned his laugh with a quiet giggle that she should have kicked her own ass for. "So, the people who almost hit her with their car seemed the obvious solution?"

"We don't know anyone else." Evan reached into his coat and pulled out a silver case. He flipped it open, and pulled out a business card. "This is our address." As Kahrin took the card, she saw Evan's eyes flick over her shoulder. "I should get back to Yelena. Please, do stop by this evening."

"Cameron!" Carbry yelled, confirming what Kahrin knew even before she turned. Innes, his nerd-sized knapsack over a shoulder, hurried on long-legged strides as soon as his eyes met hers. Even flustered and windblown, that salt and pepper hair still looked fantastic, enhancing his darkening expression. Carbry ran up from the track on exaggeratedly loping steps, bouncing on the balls of his feet. He held up a fist to bump against Innes'. "We on this week?"

Ah, yes, their weekly hot dates where Innes tutored the other boy in English. But tutoring wasn't on Innes' mind, and she could feel the unease rolling off of him from her distance away. "*Hamlet*," Innes confirmed. His eyes flicked from Carbry to Evan and back again, and he fidgeted, shifting his weight impatiently.

Kahrin waved, goodbye to Carbry and hello to Innes. She felt relieved for Innes' presence, and as soon as he could extricate himself without being rude, he quickened his steps.

"We'll talk about it," she answered Evan. It would have to do for now. "I don't drive."

"Talk about what?" Innes asked. Giant fluffy flakes accumulated on his hair and dark lashes. She supposed it was only fitting, the way the snow added some sort of ethereal quality to the one who believed in magic.

"I'll leave you to it, then," Evan said, rising to his feet with great effort. "It was nice speaking with you again, Kahrin. Innes." He inclined his head to each in turn before walking away.

Once he was out of earshot, Innes looked at Kahrin for an explanation.

"Evan wants us to babysit his sister."

Innes frowned. "Babysit."

"I can tell you on the way home." She wound her arm into his as they walked toward the parking lot, tired and worried she'd slip on the sidewalk. Of course, she did her best not to seem tired. If her parents thought she was wearing herself out, they'd make her stay home from school until she felt better. Kahrin was no honor student, but she also didn't want to miss too much class and jeopardize her graduation. Even if she was barely functioning and couldn't pay attention, she couldn't bear the thought of being home alone all day, doing nothing.

"So, he thinks I'm a bad influence on his sister?" Innes sounded offended. She couldn't fault his agitation, evident in the tightening of his jaw as he focused on driving.

Kahrin reached up, stuffing a tissue into the gap between the window and frame to make the wind stop whistling through it. Best they could do until he could get it fixed, and it wasn't enough to spare her headache. "I know, right? He doesn't even know you, and he can tell what a corrupting influence you are." She tried to underscore her attempt at levity with a salacious grin.

"Ha, ha." He glanced at her. "It's not the same thing. I can't even talk about that." He touched his stomach as if he might be sick. "I can't even think about that. Not with *her*."

Kahrin frowned. "What does that mean?"

He sighed, exasperated. "It's not a slight on you. You're not defiled or impure. I would hope you know by now that I don't believe that." She did, and shrugged, but she was agitated by it all the same. "Unicorns are . . . special. Pure. I'm not even worthy to touch her." He glanced at her. "But she can touch you."

Oh, well, that felt better. It also felt like she was overreacting, so she bit her acerbic response back and slouched down in the seat. "I know you're worried about her. This would make it easier to check on her." She looked up at him. "So we sit and talk and you do your homework. It eats up the hours you'd be freezing your nice butt off."

"Great butt."

"Great butt. Whatever," she said with a laugh. She loosened her posture a little. "Plus, he's weird. What is he, like, twenty?" She shivered. "I'll help you keep an eye on your unicorn girl, but he kind of creeps me out."

Innes smiled, making her feel silly for her spike of jealousy, and reached out an arm instead of replying. It was an answer on its own—one she understood better than words, the comfort of touch from someone you loved and trusted without thought. She slipped out of her seatbelt and scooted to the middle seat, buckling herself in and snuggling into his side.

Innes

Innes did not like this.

He didn't like that Evan Greves approached Kahrin by herself. There was something weird about an adult, however young, targeting someone underage with brain trauma and asking favors of them. Of course, Innes might just be paranoid, and that protective instinct he and Kahrin shared for one another was probably clouding his good judgment on this. Still. It bristled, both that Evan behaved as he did, and that Innes was likely being too hard on a well-intentioned man.

Or, Evan was evil and holding a unicorn hostage.

There was only one way to find out: actually go and find out. He might not like how Evan went about asking Kahrin to watch over Yelena while he was gone, but he wasn't going to turn down the opportunity to check on her. It was no real inconvenience. He'd have spent the evening with Kahrin anyhow, working on his homework while she pretended to do hers. At least this way she'd have someone else to distract when she inevitably gave up on (got bored with) her own work.

"You're quiet," Kahrin murmured. More to her knees than to herself.

"I'm quiet?" His eyes flicked sideways to her then back to the road, though one hand remained stroking her hair.

Kahrin had no hesitation in sharing exactly what she was thinking or feeling at most times, and in Innes' opinion, that was a good thing. He didn't have to guess with her in that regard. If her stomach hurt, she told him. When she wanted to fool around, she was very clear about that, too. It was the times she went quiet that troubled him. Right now was one of those times. She sat on the middle passenger seat, legs tucked beneath her, and hood of her sweatshirt pulled up with her dark hair spilling out over her shoulders. For as well as they knew one another, these were the times he almost (almost) wished he could read her thoughts.

"Do you prefer I drop you at the farm and go home?"

She shook her head. That was all the answer he was going to get. At least to that.

"Do you think he likes me? Like, like-likes me?"

Wait, what? "Who?" There were only a few options, and he knew he wasn't going to like any of them. "Carbry?"

"What? No. Don't be weird. Evan Greves. I can't tell."

With great effort, Innes managed not to sigh his exasperation. "Did you ask him?"

She shrugged one shoulder against him. "He says his interest is only in how I can help his sister."

"Okay," Innes mused. The pavement faded into the dirt roads leading toward the Quirke farm. "Here's a wild thought: He meant what he said. Hm?"

He couldn't see her face, but if he held his breath he was certain he could hear her eyes roll. "Are you saying someone like him couldn't like me?"

Storms were often preceded by tells. Signs that nature willingly offered to warn people of the impending chaos. He didn't know why, just yet, but the metaphorical birds all went silent. Either he had already, or he was about to step into the shifting winds. "Someone like what?" Clarifications were innocent, right?

Wrong. "Someone decent who seems to have his life together." So wrong. "You're not the only nice guy in existence, you know." He opened his mouth to confirm that, yes, he knew that, but the words never had a chance as she continued on. "Why wouldn't a nice guy like me?"

"Kahrin, I never said–," he started, attempting to stall what was certain to be an exciting rant. "When did the checkered flag drop?" She sat up, crossing her arms and glaring at him. There was no way this was actually about Evan Greves. "Why are we fighting?"

"Who's fighting?" she demanded. "I'm not fighting. I asked you a question, Innes. Is there something fundamental about me that would make someone like Evan Greves not like me?"

Wait, what? "Well, for one, you're seventeen. Remember?"

"So?"

"So." His hands gripped the wheel tighter. What was bothering her? "He's, well, not. He has to be, what? Twenty-two? Twenty-three?"

"Twenty-three, I think. What does that matter? It was fine in *Dirty Dancing*."

Wait, what? "No! It wasn't! You don't think that was weird? If he like-likes you, and you're a teenage girl, that doesn't bother you?"

"I'll be eighteen next year." He turned enough to see her shrug. "In a few years five years won't be so wide a gap."

"Is that your big plan? Graduate and, what? Marry Evan Greves? Punch out a few children?" Oh, please let that idea stop this nonsense.

For a moment, when she stuck out her tongue in disgust and wrinkled her nose, he thought it had. "Who said anything about getting married to anyone? Children? Are you drunk? Why is this bothering you so much? As far as I know, you and I are not planning some future together. Or did I miss something?"

Oh, that was unnecessary. She had to be doing this on purpose now. Did she really need to ask? "I don't want to see my best friend get hurt."

"Well you won't." *Wait, what?* "You're not going to be here to see all the really stupid things and people I do, are you?"

Innes signaled, despite no one being in visual distance, and steered the car to the side of the road. They were only a mile or so from the farm, but he didn't want her parents to see them fighting. That might lead to having to explain himself to her dad. He knew there was no way she was actually agitated at his doubts over Evan's attraction to her, real or perceived. "Kahrin, what's wrong? Do you actually like him?"

"No!" she burst out. As if it was the most ridiculous thing he could have said. Good. Maybe that meant they could get to the actual problem. "Maybe? He's weird. I mean, he's hot and he's nice enough." Oh, sure. "Being rich doesn't hurt. But the way he looks at me? It's like I have something he wants." She pulled her mouth into a thoughtful pucker. "I mean, maybe I do have something he wants? I don't know." She lifted and dropped her shoulders. "Fortunately I didn't have to find out what that something is because you showed up before I could find out." Aha! "Which is why I needed your opinion. I have to watch for these things myself, soon."

He leaned forward against the wheel, pressing his fingers into his eyes. "What is going on?"

"What do you mean what is going on?" She looked at him, brows lifted with the expectation that he explain himself. Oh, sure. Of the two of them, Innes was definitely the one with things to explain right now. "There's nothing going on. You're being so weird." She flopped back onto the seat, then whimpered in pain as her head hit the rest, and she rubbed at the back of it, over her hood.

Innes turned so he could put his arm around her. "You know I'm not leaving forever, right?"

She scoffed. "I know that." When Kahrin lied, a little twinge of tension gathered between her shoulder blades. Just like he felt now as he rubbed his hand over her back. "It's just college. It's not like you are going to find new and exciting things and people in a much more interesting city. Or rethink everything about your old life."

"Kahrin."

"And you know, I know how excited you are to go away and show off how brilliant you are. Then, when everyone falls in love with you–"

"Who said anything about–"

"Let me finish!" she scolded, though the little warble in

her voice betrayed her actual feelings. "When everyone falls in love with you, then you're not going to come back, leaving me stuck in this stupid place with no one around to interrupt uncomfortable conversations with possibly creepy and inappropriately older but attractive men." She took a deep breath, holding it for a moment before letting it out. "So, do you think he like-likes me? You know, so I can have some sort of base by which to judge people."

Affection tipped one side of his smile further up than the other. "First of all, of course I'll come back. Pickle chews the sofa when he gets bored. Imagine what you'll do!" She let a soft snort, trying to pretend that wasn't funny. "Secondly, no one will ever love me like my best friend." The chest strap of his seatbelt whined as he leaned to bump his nose against hers. "Just like no one will love her like I do. And," he stole a quick kiss and sat up, "you could always come visit me."

She swiped at him, as he knew she would, but missed, because he planned ahead. "You know I can't drive."

He shrugged. "True, though you could learn. You have to eventually, right?"

"Only because you're leaving." She huffed, which quickly became a yawn. She was going to need a nap before they went out again. Since she would never admit she needed a nap, he'd have to distract her until she dozed off. Luckily, he was experienced in such subterfuge. "I don't have a luxury ride such as this, either." She lifted her hands as if she was helpless to do anything.

He smiled, chucked her under the chin before he eased back onto the road. After checking all of his blind spots, of course. "Well, you've got me there."

CHAPTER FIVE

Kahrin

It was the next afternoon when Innes turned the car onto the paved town roads, the sound of the tires smoothing into a quiet hum. Or, as quiet as anything could be when every single sound shoved pins through your skull, which Kahrin felt keenly now. The GPS guided them around several back roads, an oddly roundabout route, until finally directing them to the right driveway. How had they lived in this stupid town their whole stupid lives and had no memory of this house existing? The older style was not entirely incongruous with the rest of the houses around it, with their little walkways on top and tower things, though the others had been updated with vinyl siding and other touches that Da was always talking about doing but didn't want to pay someone else to do. The Greves' house was in need of a scrape-and-paint, though the pretty leaded windows on the front sparkled.

They both climbed out of the driver's side door, Kahrin even suffering Innes' hand up and out, and walked slowly up to the house.

"Anytime you want to leave," he reminded her, "just say the word."

She knew which one, "*vigil*," and nodded her agreement. Ever since they were very young, pretending to camp on the back porch and sitting vigil to watch for monsters, it was a signal of trust between them. No matter what was going on—whether they had scared themselves with stories, or fooling around had gone a direction one or both of them did not find comfortable—either of them could say it, and the other would know to stop whatever they were doing. She had not said it now, and swatted at him. "I'm fine. Stop fussing."

His mouth hooked up on one side. "You telling me to stop fussing usually makes me stop fussing, hm?" He wrapped her up in his arms and nuzzled into her neck, making her giggle and squirm.

"Stop it." He wouldn't, she knew, but she had a duty to pretend it bugged her. Which it did not.

They rang the bell, one of those old ones that sounded old-fashioned with the stereotypical *ding-dong*. Almost a full minute passed, where Kahrin bounced on her toes to expel her unspent energy, before the sound of steps approached. The door with the large stained glass panel swung inward, revealing Evan Greves, wavy blond hair swept back and blue eyes crinkled.

"Kahrin," Evan greeted her warmly before turning a nod to Innes, greeting him with a low utterance of his name. It didn't take a genius to figure out that Innes was not wanted here. Since she wasn't a genius, she had to rely on their earlier conversation to put that one together. Evan's attempts to get Kahrin here alone seemed to have Innes on edge, given the way the tendon in his jaw tightened. She was still undecided in her opinion. "I'm so glad you decided to come tonight."

Evan stepped back, gesturing them into the house through a small entryway. Innes let her go first, as he was wont to do with his fussy manners. As soon as they stepped over the threshold, where they shed their shoes and coats, he shivered. He paused, just for a heartbeat, before moving on.

"What's wrong?" she asked, grasping his arm.

His brows drew together. "Just a weird feeling." He rubbed at the back of his neck.

Before she could prod him further on it, Evan interrupted, walking between them as if he expected the path to be clear. "Sister, we have company." When no answer came, either words or movement, he called out again as he ushered them into the living room. At least, it looked like a living room, if you weren't expected to sit on the furniture. This was definitely not the Quirke farmhouse, and no one would be propping their feet on the gleaming coffee table or tucking their legs beneath them on the white sofa. Who had a white sofa? Apparently, Evan and Yelena Greves, but judging how the former lowered himself onto it, the purpose of it was very much for sitting. "Don't be rude, Yelena," Evan rebuked her, adjusting himself in his seat.

Yelena drifted in from another room, which Kahrin couldn't see beyond a hardwood staircase with an ornately carved rail and spindles. If Yelena had been preceded with a tinkle of wind chimes, Kahrin would not have been surprised. As it was, she was haloed with a confetti of colored light falling from tall stained glass windows, and it didn't look out of place. Innes, predictably, could not have been more astonished, judging by the way his mouth gaped. Yelena floated on nearly silent steps, like she decided where to go and suddenly she was there. Innes sucked in a breath, audibly, as she turned to meet his eyes.

Yes, yes, she was pretty. Big deal. Except, even Kahrin had to admit she was more than pretty. She was like, unreal, in a way. Her eyes were just a little too far apart, her neck almost too thin to hold her head up, and somehow she was all the more elegant for it. Being pretty wasn't odd, though. What really stood out was how she seemed so sad. No, not just sad. Even Kahrin's chest squeezed to look at her, though Innes appeared as if the simple act of looking upon her caused grief in his heart he could not bear. Great.

"It's nice to see you again," she greeted them, her voice ethereal and far off, like she called to them from a dream and could only pay some of her attention. Her hands folded very primly in front of her, the cuffs of a fluffy lavender sweater almost swallowing them. She smiled, but it neither reached her eyes nor did anything to put anyone at ease.

Kahrin waved her fingers from where they lay, crossed over her arm. "Hey."

"Kahrin has agreed to stay with you while I'm out. Her *friend*," there was a way Evan paused over the word that struck Kahrin as odd, "will evidently stay with her."

"I don't mind," Innes insisted. "It's the least we can do, since the accident."

Yelena looked from Kahrin, to Innes, and back again. "It was no accident."

Wait, what?

"Yelena," Evan scolded, his voice barely audible, yet like drizzled chocolate. Subtle, sweet, but firm all the same. She turned her eyes downward, and Kahrin saw Innes' hands curl into fists. "We talked about this."

"Yes, Evan. I'm sorry." She looked between the pair of them again, her eyes fixing intently, first upon Kahrin, then, with a frown, meeting his. Innes seemed as if it was too much to bear, and he looked away.

A moment later, Innes' head snapped up, meeting Yelena's eyes again. His brows lifted, enough that Kahrin noticed, but only because she knew his face by heart. Innes looked around the room, trying to source some sound that could not be heard, and once again, his attention was drawn back to Yelena.

Kahrin felt her brow crease. She knew she was missing something, some inside joke that passed between her best friend and someone who was not her. She frowned.

Innes' deep, dark eyes widened, and Yelena shook her head, nearly imperceptibly. Kahrin barely noticed. But she did.

Innes cleared his throat. "It's been a long drive. Could we trouble you for some water?" Kahrin looked at him, her mouth moving to protest. "I promised your mother I wouldn't let you get dehydrated." *What?* She understood not to argue, even if she didn't know what he was talking about.

"Of course," Evan replied, his grip on his cane shifting so he could stand.

"Please," Innes interrupted, mildly, with a lift of his hand. "Don't get up. Just point us to the kitchen."

Evan lofted a hand in the direction of the dining room. "Just on the other side."

Innes grabbed Kahrin by the hand and led her out of the room, guiding her around the antique table and chairs. Once they were in the kitchen, he made sure they were out of sight of the door.

Kahrin pulled her hand away and looked at him. "I'm not thirsty." The little crease of his brow was all she needed to know this was not about hydration.

"Tell me you heard it." Kahrin looked at him, her eyes blank with confusion. She lifted her hands in question. What was he going on about? He shook his head, remembering her concussion. "Yelena."

Kahrin scrubbed at her face, already tired, and sure there was not going to be rest anytime soon. "I don't know what you're talking about. Hear what?"

"She needs our help." His fingers grasped her elbow, an earnestness on his face she knew was going to talk her into whatever he was planning. "She told me she needs our help."

"She told you?" Kahrin's eyes went from confused to worried. Were they sure he hadn't hit his head in the crash? "What do you mean she told you?"

"I heard her ask us for help. She's in trouble, Kahrin."

"From what? A rich, overdressed, slightly weird brother who wants to take care of her?" she asked as she flung her arms into the air and let them drop to her sides.

"Something's not right here, Kahrin. He's not her brother."

Oh, good grief. "Of course he's her brother." She shoved her hands into her hair, already knowing they were barreling toward a fight. "Innes, what's going on?"

"I think she's trapped here," he insisted.

Kahrin knew him better than anyone and wanted to believe him. What he wanted her to believe, however, was absurd. "Trapped how?" she hissed, afraid of being overheard by their hosts. "She's not chained up. She's walking around just fine. The door wasn't even locked when we got here."

"I think he's using magic to keep her here." Oh, no. "Maybe that's why she can't remember what she is." She

63

didn't want to fight. She knew he believed Yelena to be unicorn and wanted to work together to help her. And to work together, he needed Kahrin to believe what he knew to be certain. "Can't you feel it? I felt a chill when we came inside."

"A chill? In January? You don't say!" She took a deep breath and let it out. She could see in his eyes that he knew she wanted to believe him, if for no other reason than it was him and her. "This house is, like, a bajillion-years old. Of course you felt a chill. So, what do you want to do? Should I hit him over the head while you princess-carry her to the car?"

Innes rolled his eyes. "I don't know yet, but we have to get her out of here." He clasped Kahrin's shoulders lightly with both hands. "She's in danger, and he knows that I know." *Wait, what?* "That's why he doesn't want me here."

"Why would he invite us here if he was going to hurt her? I'm tired, and I don't want to have a row right now, in someone else's home." Her eyes closed for a moment, then fluttered open.

She saw the pang of guilt flit across his face. She was still recovering, and he was browbeating her with all of this. "I don't want to fight, either. I just. . . . I know I'm right. I heard her beg for help. I think it's this house." He ran a hand over his hair, messing it out of that carefully styled-to-be-not-styled-at-all look. "Please trust me. I need you to trust me."

Part of her was absolutely certain she would dig her heels in and refuse. In fact, she hoped she would. Instead, her expression softened, and she nodded without realizing she'd done it. "Okay. I like them. I trust you. You know I do."

"Thank you," he said, pulling her into a hug. She wrapped her arms about him and nodded. She couldn't really deny him something he believed so ardently. Innes believed nothing without reason for it. "We need to get them apart."

"I don't like where this is going," she grumbled against his chest before he released her.

Innes sighed, filling a glass near the sink with water so it at least looked like they'd come in here for a reason. "I don't either, but what choice do we have?"

Kahrin took the glass from his hand, agitation spiking again. "Obviously, we don't." She turned on her heel and walked back to the living room without looking to see if he followed, using each step to find a way to put a friendly look back on her face as she did.

Innes

He didn't want to fight, and Kahrin's concussion made her more easily agitated than normal. Given that her moods already turned on a hairpin, that was saying something. She practically marched, heavy steps on wooden floors, back to the sitting room, strain pulling the corners of her mouth. What could he do but follow? He brought the glass of water to maintain the pretense, and also because Kahrin honestly needed it.

"I trust everything is alright?" Evan asked. Though his smile was bland, his yellowed eyes flicked to Innes and back to Kahrin again. "I worried you might have gotten lost."

"Just ducky," Kahrin answered, a little too convincing to be true. "I was admiring your . . . crown . . ." She pointed at the ceiling, making circles with her finger as she stalled for a word that seemed just outside her reach. "Windows. You have all these fancy windows."

Crown windows? It was all he could do not to groan, and hope they weren't thrown out. "She really likes architecture."

"Mostly ceilings," she supplied, "as recently I've spent a lot of time comparing them." Innes pressed his lips together as he tried to keep his cheeks from warming. She wouldn't blatantly betray his privacy, but she'd use enough entendre to prickle him. "But your windows are so pretty."

Yelena looked between them; when her eyes met his it sent a chill through him. He could hardly stand the gravity of that fleeting connection, the weight of her gaze causing a swaying sensation. In that moment, she could have blamed anything on him, and he'd have questioned his own innocence. Somehow, turning the same look upon Kahrin did not have the same effect. However she was able to resist that feeling, he didn't know, both envying her ignorance and grieving her loss of it.

"I've had little to do apart from assessing the windows. There's some lovely dormers in the attic," Yelena said as she rose from her seat, water flowing in reverse. "The leaded glass is original, I believe." She glanced to Evan, and Innes thought he saw a sharp glimmer of defiance in her eyes.

A strange stiffness fell between the four of them, as though each of them were waiting for one of the others to protest the idea of the girls going to the attic. It didn't come, so Kahrin stood with a strained smile. "That sounds nice." Her eyes flicked to Innes and then to Evan and back again, looking for one of them to object.

"Be careful on the stairs," Innes told her. Yes, that was the big worry right now, but what else could he say? It served them well if she went with Yelena so Innes could talk to Evan. Innes' hands balled into fists just at the way the man looked at them, something close to hunger on his face. It was dark and at odds with the smile he maintained. Perhaps Yelena was not the only one in danger here.

"Whatever you say." Despite Kahrin's light tone, her words still felt sharp. Maybe it was that tense smile she wore.

She followed Yelena to the exquisite hardwood stairs, lined with a rug held in place on each step with an iron rod. Even though Kahrin was far from clumsy in movement, she looked as much next to the unicorn-turned-girl who all but floated away with steps that didn't make so much as a scuff on the rug.

Evan rose to his feet, leaning his weight upon the cane. "I could accompany you, if it would make your friend feel better." Innes did not care for the way he spoke about, and rarely to, him, as if he was not there or inconsequential. Maybe he was imagining it, or maybe there really was something predatory in Mr. Greves' expression. Either way, Innes felt his jaw tighten as he fought against his temper. That was the last thing they needed. So, how did he keep Evan from being alone with the girls without making it into an ordeal?

"You know," Innes started, pausing because he had no further plan beyond interrupting Evan's attempts to follow the girls to the attic. "I've never been in a house this old before." He turned about, feigning interest in the structure. "I wouldn't mind a tour, either."

Stop interfering.

Innes blinked, his attention focused on Evan. What was that? The man's face remained impassive, giving no indication one way or the other. Innes took a slow, quiet breath, willing his agitation away. That would make twice today he heard voices that no one else seemed to notice.

"Then we can join the ladies at the top and work our way down." Greves started after the girls, giving Innes no recourse.

So, up the stairs they went. They paused at a small landing so Kahrin could admire the towering leaded windows that scattered polychromatic light on everything it touched, including her pretty face and large, doll-like eyes. When she was satisfied, they turned to proceed upward to the next floor. The whole pattern repeated before turning them toward the attic. They took each step slowly as Kahrin took her time climbing up to the spacious attic.

Did whatever Evan was doing work both ways? If people could put thoughts in his head, could they also read his? Just because Innes believed in the existence of magic didn't mean he fully understood the ins and outs of how it worked. Innes brought up the rear, his steps heavier and slower as he turned this over in his mind. If he thought something, really hard, would they be able to hear it? There was only one way to find out, hm?

What if I pushed you down the stairs? It wasn't so hard to put a boost behind it, his protective instinct strong. Or so he thought. Truthfully, he had no idea how one thought hard. He gritted his teeth, eyes squinting at the back of Evan's head as if he could bore the thought through his skull with his glare. *I know what she is.*

If it had any effect, Evan did not react to it. They arrived in the attic without fanfare, Yelena showing Kahrin the little half-circle windows, as promised. The late sunlight sprinkled a mosaic of colors across the wooden floor: watery greens and vibrant reds, assisted by cobalt blues and pinkish browns. They twinkled across the beams, and, if he held his breath, he swore he could hear the cartoonish sound of a spell being cast.

"Goodness, I always forget how much junk we've accumulated." Evan began moving things around with a low, oily chuckle. Okay, maybe that was just Innes' bias speaking, but the man was sinister and obviously up to an evil plan, and Innes would prove it.

"My ma says things breed when you leave them in storage and don't check back to make sure they're leaving room for the Lord." Kahrin called over her shoulder, her voice cheery. Evan laughed that soft, slimy laugh again. Which Kahrin seemed to enjoy. Great!

"It's strange," Innes mused. "You say you've been here a long time, but I don't think I've ever met you before." There were a lot of strange things about the Greveses, but that fact stood out the most in his mind, just then. It was not a large town. Ma Quirke knew the dinner times of almost every family just so she could catch them at home if she needed to. How had he lived here for this long and never met the Greveses?

"Sometimes we fail to notice things we see every day," Evan answered quietly, his voice pitched for only Innes to hear. His gaze settled upon Kahrin and Yelena, making stiff conversation over something they obviously had no interest in. Innes couldn't tell what Evan's interest was in Kahrin, especially when he had an actual unicorn hostage in his home. Surely he was not actually going to make a move on her?

Evan cursed suddenly, softly, lifting his hand to examine it. "Clumsy of me," he said, as calmly as if he'd simply dropped a pen or his cane. Sure enough, a bloody gash scored, red and angry, across his palm. Innes couldn't even see what he'd cut it on. There didn't appear to be anything sharper than the lid of the storage container he moved. His eyes hard on Innes, Evan closed his fist over the wound, and it glowed a coruscating green, multihued and opalescent.

I warned you.

The air prickled, faint, but there, like the moment immediately after a strike of lightning when everything seemed a little charged. It lifted the hairs on his neck and arms, and from the other side of the room he heard the heartbreaking sound of Yelena gasping in fear.

Kahrin, her attention on the patterned glass, whipped around at the sound, her large, mismatched eyes narrowed with confusion. Had she really not noticed what the rest of them clearly did?

"No. No, no." Yelena backed up slowly, bumping against a stack of packed wooden crates used for storing fragile items. "Please, Evan." Her voice, that dreamy quality gone, replaced by a knife's edge of horror. It sank straight through Innes' sternum, sticking there, stifling his breath.

"What?" Kahrin looked between them, frowning. "What's wrong?"

"What are you doing to her?" Innes demanded as he stepped forward and grabbed Evan's wrist. "He's cut himself." Why? He didn't know, but he knew what he saw. Knew what he felt. There was a connection there, and he couldn't explain how, but he just *knew.*

The green glow vanished and the charge through the air stilled. Evan stepped back, twisting his hand out of Innes' grip, his words sharp with offense. "What are you talking about? Let go of me."

"Innes, what's wrong with you?" Kahrin demanded.

Evan opened his hand, displaying the smooth skin of his palm. There was no cut! For all anyone could see, it had never been there. No scar. No mark. "If I had cut myself, wouldn't there be a cut?"

Kahrin walked closer, craning to see Evan's hand, but Yelena backed up against the wall, pulling at her hair and whimpering. Kahrin glanced up at him. "He's fine."

"He wasn't fine a minute ago! Don't you see?" He pointed. "He cut himself and then healed it. I could feel the magic."

"Magic?" Evan exclaimed, his throat turning the words into a chuckle. "What's this all about?" He looked at Kahrin. "There's no such thing."

"Liar!" Yelena screamed. She shook her head, the mane of her cascading curls tossing about on her shoulders and back. "You're lying, and he knows it!" She hovered against the wall, pointing at Innes.

"See?" Innes looked at Kahrin and pointed at Evan. "I told you something was going on here." Kahrin's eyes narrowed, her expression going dark.

Yelena rushed across the room toward Innes. He took an equal number of steps back to keep the space between them. No matter how he longed to protect her, he could not let her touch him. He just couldn't! He needn't have worried; as if a barrier existed between them, she came to a halt and would step no closer. "Please. Please help me. He's not my brother. He's done something to me!" Her voice rose with every syllable, cracking at the epoch.

"Yelena, calm yourself," Evan cooed, every bit the concerned caretaker.

"Innes!" He could not have missed the disappointment in Kahrin's voice if he'd been trying to ignore it. It stung that she didn't believe him, and he flinched. "What are you doing?"

"What am I doing? What's he done?" he asked Yelena, desperation straining his words as he continued pointing at Evan in accusation.

"That's enough!" Evan bellowed. They all froze, looking to Evan Greves, the man who barely spoke above a whispering wind. "Kahrin, I knew this was a poor decision. Your," that pause again as he gritted his teeth through the next word, "*friend* is feeding my sister's theatrics."

"Stop lying!" Yelena shrieked out. "He's lying! Innes he's lying. You know I'm telling the truth." She turned to Kahrin in a desperate plea. "Please. You have to believe me!" Her words choked off in a terrified sob and she crouched to the ground, rocking back and forth on bent knees and clutching at her brow.

Evan stepped closer to Yelena. "Now look what you've done." She backed up, skidding on her rear and feet, shaking her head and holding one hand up defensively. He stopped a pace short of her, his voice taking on that sing-song condescension people use with upset children. "It's okay, sister, dear. They're leaving."

"No!" she shrieked. "No, don't go!" Her clear-blue eyes, wild with fright, caught Innes', leaving a pain in his heart that stopped his breath.

"Kahrin," Evan started, sounding beleaguered and exhausted. "I do apologize for such an impolite dismissal, but you and your friend must leave." He looked to Innes, eyes narrowed, and an odd twitch to the corner of his mouth. He hid it well, but he was happy for this outburst. "You are no longer welcome in our home, Mister Cameron."

I warned you not to interfere.

Kahrin rubbed at her temple with one hand. "I'm so sorry, Evan," she muttered, another verbal strike that made Innes flinch. "I was wrong. We're going. Right, Innes?" She shot a look at Innes as she stomped for the stairs, leaving him gaping.

Despite Yelena's heart-wrenching pleas, he followed Kahrin's slow progression down the stairs, giving the frightened girl an apologetic look as he left her alone with this man who was certainly not her brother, and who had certainly used magic. He knew it.

He would be back. He would find a way.

CHAPTER SIX

Innes

Giving Kahrin space was generally the best idea when she was angry. She was far less likely to throw something at you if you weren't there to have it thrown at you. So that was exactly what Innes did; he waited a whole day. She didn't come to school, which was not so surprising given how difficult her recovery had been, but it still worried him. So, he went to class. He ate lunch with Carbry, who seemed less chatty in Kahrin's absence. He checked his phone between classes to see if she'd called or texted, which she did not. With no small amount of willpower, he didn't contact her either.

Instead, he went around to her teachers after school to collect her assignments, certainly not as an excuse to drive out to the Quirke farm to see her. Since he'd gone to all the trouble to collect them for her, what was the harm in taking them to her?

She couldn't stay mad at him forever! Not for something that wasn't his fault. Innes knew what he saw just as certain as Kahrin knew what she did not see. He practiced what he was going to say the whole ride out, though none of it seemed good enough to make up for the fact that he'd gotten them thrown out of the Greves' house. It also seemed unlikely she was going to forgive him anytime soon for implying her concussion might have been affecting her perception. Stranger things had happened, though, like voices in his head and magically healing injuries.

When he pulled in the drive she was outside. Bundled up in a barn jacket and thick hat, she chased around an escaped goat, one of the bucks that always seemed to find his way out, no matter how many times or how the fence was secured. Pickle helped her wrangle it back to the pen. He pulled into his spot by the pen and waved, smiling hopefully. He knew she saw him, and she knew he knew she saw him. She turned back to the pen as if she hadn't, winding the fencing shut.

"Hey," he called to her as he climbed out of the newly repaired car. The paint was still scraped and unlikely to be redone anytime soon, but at least the doors on both sides worked!

Kahrin paused to look at him, then made a quick kissing noise to Pickle as she turned to go back to the house. Pickle trotted excitedly by her side, turning about now and then to give an excited woof to Innes, urging him to hurry up. "I'm not speaking to you," she hollered over her shoulder.

The corner of his mouth hooked upward, helplessly. "Isn't that talking to me?" he asked as he jogged in long, loping strides to follow her.

"Starting right now." If he hadn't known better, he'd have thought she could feel the twitch of his smile. "I mean, that doesn't count! Starting right now."

"Okay." He caught up to her, though he stayed well out of arm's reach. The farm truck was gone. So was Brecken's motorcycle. "Don't talk." He held out the grocery sack he'd stuffed her books and assignments into. "So you don't get bored."

That stopped her. She looked at the bag of books as if he was offering her a rat. "I'm not that bored."

"That counts as talking."

Oh, she was mad, but she was also amused. She tucked her full lips and bit down to hide the starting of a grin and opened the mudroom door, letting Pickle run ahead of them. "Stop that."

Innes affected innocence. "Stop what?"

"That charming best friend shit." She sat on the bench inside the door and fumbled to get her boots off. "I'm still mad at you." Feet freed of their confines, she kicked the boots under the bench with her heels.

"I know."

"Then why are you here?" She looked up at him, her mouth pulled to one side.

Kicking off one boot and then the other, Innes put them beside hers under the bench and offered her a hand up to standing. "I wanted to apologize."

"You already did that," she reminded him. "I didn't accept." She glanced at the grocery sack of schoolwork again. "I don't think that's going to change my mind."

"No, I didn't think so." He followed her through the dining area and past the large table. "Plus, I miss you." The living room still held the obvious terrain of her couch fort: a trail of blankets, the couch pillows piled up on one end, and the remains of snacks littered about on dirty dishes. "How are you feeling?"

She swept one of the quilts up from the davenport and swung it around her shoulders, cocooning herself. "Tired, mostly. I've had a headache so bad all day I could barely move. It only just eased so I could go outside."

"Were you supposed to be chasing the goats?" He tilted his head, worry creasing his brows. The roll of her eyes answered that. He sat on the couch beside her and held up an arm in offer. She did her due diligence in resisting, pretending that it was some great consideration before letting the most put-upon sigh and sliding under it. "I am sorry."

She shrugged. "I know. I know you are. I just . . ." He tensed waiting for whatever was coming. "Look, I know you believe in all that . . . unicorn and magic stuff." She turned her mismatched hazel eyes up to meet his. "You know I'd do anything for you."

He nodded. She'd proven that more than a few times over. She had a scar on her left shoulder, a trophy for that willingness to support even his wildest antics. Like when they'd scaled the barn roof because he thought wishes had a better chance of coming true if you were closer to the stars. He wasn't sure the boxer's fracture in her carpals ever healed from the many, many punches she threw when kids teased him for his clothes or storybooks.

"Evan won't speak to me," she started, and when he opened his mouth to argue, she held up a finger to quiet him. "I know you don't like him, and you don't have to. I do. Maybe."

"I don't trust him. There's something wrong with him." Innes could feel his fingers ball into fists. "He's using you."

"How?" she demanded. He winced as she pulled away and stood up from the davenport. "How is the nice man who just wants a friend for his sister using me?" She stomped away from the couch. "Oh, right, because my head's all messed up. So he's gonna use me! For what?"

"I don't know!" He couldn't sit anymore, and pushed

up to his feet. "He wants something from you. He looks at you strangely." Like he would consume her if given the chance. There was no interpretation of that thought that didn't send blood roaring in his ears.

"Strangely?" Kahrin shook her head. "You mean, like I'm a pretty girl? What is this, Innes? Are you *jealous*?"

"What? No!" He ran a hand over the back of his neck. "Not like that."

"No, I know. It's *not like that*." She rubbed at her eyes and pulled at the long braid of her hair. "It's not like anything."

What did that mean? "Kahrin."

"No! You listen to me. Yelena is a scared and sick girl. I know you think she's something else."

"A unicorn," he reiterated firmly.

"Yes. And I want to believe you. You know I do. I love you." She gestured wildly at the bay window to indicate their trip to the Greveses' home. "You can't behave like that!"

"I saw him cut himself and then heal it, Kahrin. His hand was green! I know what I saw. I felt it. Yelena felt it."

She let a grunt of aggravation. "Yelena, Yelena, Yelena! I wish she was a unicorn so we could fight about something else. What is it with her?"

"You know what it is. What she is. She needs our help. I know she does." He lifted both brows. "Are *you* jealous?"

She blinked. "No!" She scoffed and crossed her arms, looking anywhere but at him.

Wait, what? "Kahrin, you know that–"

"Yes. I know. It's not like that, and I promise, it's not like that, it's just . . .," she grunted in frustration. "You're my best friend. I've known you longer than I haven't. You know everything about me, and I don't know where you end and I begin." She bobbed her head to the side knowingly. "In more ways than one, now. And you're leaving me."

"Not for months yet." He stepped closer, careful not to trip over the pile of blankets and beanbag chairs. He grabbed her hands. "That's so far off."

"No. No it's not." Every now and then she looked at him in a way that hurt so deeply he didn't know what to do with the feeling. She did so now. "When you add up all the months of our lives, what's left is hardly anything at all." She shrugged and pulled her hands away. "You're smart, and you're gonna go off to that fancy university and be something super great. Who knows if I'll ever see you again."

"Of course you will," he insisted, using the pad of his thumb to wipe a tear from her cheek. Watching her cry never got easier, especially when he knew he was causing the tears. "You could go away to that fancy university, too, you know."

She waved a dismissive hand, as she was wont to do when they had this conversation.

"You're going to spend all the time we have left worrying about Yelena, trying to be a storybook hero, and I'm going to feel like a selfish ass who gets jealous because you get a girlfriend."

"That is not going to happen." If that's what this was, it was easy to fix. "I can't be with her. Not . . ." The idea was so horrifying that he trailed off. "Kahrin, she's a unicorn. I told you, she's immortal."

He could tell she didn't quite believe him, but she was giving him the benefit of the doubt. "So, you're not going to . . ." She circled her fingers in front of her. If it was him struggling, she'd never stop taunting him about not being able to utter the word 'sex'.

"No. No, I couldn't if I wanted to. Don't you listen when I tell you stories?" He leaned down to draw her into a brief kiss. "You're my best friend." He bumped her cheek with his nose, smiling hopefully that the fight was behind them. "And I promise, you get first dibs on my time."

"After your stupid books." She smiled, and the squeeze in his chest eased. Fighting was never easy. It ate at them both in ways he couldn't explain, and couldn't bear. "Can I have some of your time right now?" she asked with that drop in her voice she'd learned to use way too quickly. She slipped her arms around his waist, and he wrapped his around her to pull her closer. Tipping up on her toes, she leaned to resume that kiss from a moment ago. One he was happy to indulge for just a moment.

"Have I ever mentioned how hard it is to keep up with you?" He rested his forehead against hers.

"Only every day that I've known you." She grinned and butted her head against his lightly, though not light enough to avoid a flash of pain. "However, it has been worse since you ruined my maidenhood."

He snorted, almost choking on it. "That's exactly how I remember it." Bumping her nose once more, he retracted one of his arms and reached into his pocket. "Before we get carried away and I forget." He pressed a set of keys into her hand, attached to a carved keychain that didn't really look like anything, despite his best efforts. "Happy birthday."

She looked from the keys to him and back again. "What's this?"

"Keys to my car."

"No." She shook her head and held up the keychain. "This."

He felt his cheeks warm. "Brodie tried to teach me to whittle. I'm not very good at it."

She snorted. "You don't say. What are these for?"

He shrugged. "I won't need it after I leave. I thought, maybe, you'd want to use it."

"I don't know how to drive, Pretty Mouth." The crease of her brow deepened.

He lifted and dropped his shoulders. "I guess we know how we'll be filling our time."

"One way, anyway." She gave him a little punch to the arm and chuckled. Something still seemed off, but she apparently decided to set it aside for now. She put the keys in her own pocket, and drove him back to the davenport with a barrage of playful little punches.

Kahrin

People liked to talk about The First Time. As if it were some special holiday that you'd mark on your calendar and celebrate every year for the rest of your stupid boring life. Those were the people who cautioned you that you shouldn't give it to just anyone, as if sex was a gift you bestowed on someone for not being an utter ass.

Kahrin did not agree.

She'd been lucky, of course. The First Time had been the result of an incredibly boring summer day. Innes was doing summer classes at the Community College (nerd alert) and sat on the davenport fixated with whatever seemed appropriate to take up his free time. Kahrin lay on the floor, her hair spread out and legs up on the couch. She tried to focus her attention on a book, but she'd read the same paragraph three times and still didn't know what it was about. The heat was oppressive, and despite having all the windows and doors in the farmhouse thrown open, even her spandex running shorts and sports bra were too stifling.

So, she did what any other bored teenager would do, she reasoned. She clicked her tongue in thought, breaking the silence as she often did before suggesting some shenanigan or another that Innes would either try to talk her out of, or wouldn't. He didn't, and as things turned out, they both viewed it as a transaction of sorts: You make me feel good, I make you feel good, and everyone's happy. It changed nothing between them beyond the fact that now they had one more thing to do when there was nothing to do (but each other).

Which meant it did not feel weird at all that after their fight, such as it was, Kahrin playfully batted her fists at her best friend until he flopped onto the davenport. She oh so clumsily fell into his lap, and one thing led to another because who didn't want to help their best friend feel better after a fight? Honestly, it would have been selfish to do otherwise!

Something stuck in the back of her mind, though. Some niggling thought she couldn't get rid of, no matter whose lips were where or whose hands gripped what. It had nothing to do with Evan or Yelena, whom she quickly shoved out of her mind for the moment because she *did not share*. She wrapped herself up in the here and the now, not wanting to think about anything else. Which was probably why she didn't hear the truck pull in. When the door to the mudroom opened, she let out a frustrated squeal and hopped off Innes faster than she left a starting block.

"Well hello, you two," Ma greeted them as she poked into the den. She looked at Kahrin, wrapped in a blanket, and Innes, who'd moved to sitting on the floor with his knees pulled up to his chest.

Innes cleared his throat. "Good evening, Mrs. Quirke."

"Hungry?" The corners of her mouth twitched as she looked between them, and Kahrin knew she was not fooled for even a second, with their flushed faces and kiss-swollen lips. "You kids work up such appetites."

"No, ma'am. Thank you." He did his best not to look at her.

Kahrin bit her lower lip to avoid laughing at the red of Innes' face, which only darkened when Da walked into the room behind Ma, face impassive as he looked directly at him. "You'll stay for dinner." Da's word was final on it, as far as he was concerned, and he tromped out of the dining room. "I told Alec to muck that pen."

"I did it," Kahrin called after him. "I was bored."

"Kahrin," Ma scolded. "You're supposed to be resting. I'm sure you can find better things to do with your boredom." She nodded to the two of them. "Innes." Then left them alone.

Now, the transaction only worked if everyone got what they bargained for. Kahrin twitched and squirmed around, agitated with energy to spare and nowhere to spend it. Most of the irritation from their fight quickly replaced itself with annoyance at this interruption.

"Come on," she grumbled, pushing up from the floor and leaving the room, her heavy footfalls reminiscent of

Da's as she did.

It didn't take Innes long to be on his feet and following after her. They had a lot of practice springing to action at one or the other's whims. "Where are you going?"

"To try out my new keys." There was an edge to her voice she did not expect, but did not stop to think on it. She shoved her feet into sneakers and was out the door before she had her barn coat in both hands. "Gotta make the best of the time, I guess."

"Should you be driving with a concussion?" he inquired as he hopped down the deck steps behind her.

She knew in her heart of hearts that he did not mean to irritate her with the question. "If I pass out at the wheel you can just wake me up." She fished the keyring from her jeans pocket and twirled them by the adorably disfigured carved keychain. "Or take the wheel."

"That's not how that works," he said, long strides catching up with her before she reached the car. He grasped her by the elbow. "Kahrin, what's wrong?"

She turned about, pulling her elbow free and walking the last few steps to the car backward, something squeezing in her chest as she held his eyes. "Why would you say something's wrong?"

"Oh, I don't know. Years of practice?"

"I just want to try out my new birthday present!" The false cheer in her voice caught even her off guard, but she wasn't going to spend much time thinking about it. She slid into the driver's seat, fumbling around for the latch to move the seat until she could pull the bench forward. "Have your legs always been this damned long?" she asked, trying to be breezy. The problem with trying to be breezy was that it undid the breezy part.

She started the car before Innes was even in his seat, hastily buckling his seatbelt. She heard the deep breath in and then out as he strained to stay calm. "When's the last time you drove?"

"I took the tractor down the road to the field to hitch it to the tiller after harvest." How different could it be? Innes' little K-car had way more mirrors than Da's tractor, and weighed a lot less. Especially without the tiller.

"If I'd known you were going to try this right away, I'd have backed in so you don't have to–"

He quieted as the car jerked backward, then slammed to a stop as she overcompensated. "Sorry." She winced, and put the car into drive. This time she eased more carefully onto the gas, and turned them toward the road.

"What's wrong?" he repeated.

"Nothing's wrong, other than your brakes being too damned touchy."

He growled, but not in that fun way she enjoyed. "Stop lying to me."

Ouch. She tugged her lip in with her teeth, concentrating. "I'm not trying to." Once on the dirt road, she accelerated, gradually at first. By the time they passed the field she'd picked up a good speed. It wasn't exactly the same as running, with the wind biting her face and her legs pumping in concert with the rest of her body, but it would do. "I don't know what's wrong."

"Then let's talk through it." His fingers curled around the oh-shit bar above the door.

"There's nothing to talk about. Whatever's wrong is my problem, not yours."

"Since when?"

Now it was her turn to growl. "Just let it alone."

"You know I can't do that."

"Can't or won't, Innes?"

"Pick one."

Her foot hit the brake harder than she meant it to, and she veered quickly to the side of the road, bringing them to a fairly rough stop. She put the car in park, then held the wheel until her knuckles whitened. "You just can't wait to leave, can you?"

"What?" Oh, come on, he was not confused. "What are you talking about?"

"Your keys. The car. All this talk about time left and next year? You never miss a chance to remind me that *you're* leaving, and that I'm going to be stuck all alone in this stupid town with no way out."

"Kahrin–," he started.

She had no patience to wait for him to finish. "The worst part? I want you to go. I want you to get the hell out of Brodie's house so you can have your own space with your own bookshelves to put all your silly books on." She slumped back in the seat, arms crossing over her chest. "Of course I want what's best for you, no matter how it hurts. But you don't have to keep rubbing it in my face."

"I'm not trying to rub anything in your face. You know, you could get out of here, too, if you tried. Come live with me in the city."

Kahrin laughed, the bitterness cutting but keeping her tears at bay. "What am I going to do? There's no pens to muck in the city, and I'm not smart like you."

"That's not true. You're smart in different ways." Bless his heart for trying to make her feel better.

"You're right." She laughed, the sound almost frantic. "There's probably a lot out there for me with my sprint times, deep knowledge of impregnating goats, and tractor repair." She glanced over at him. "I'm probably going to be pregnant in a bus station inside a year, so that'll help."

"Kahrin," he said again, this time sounding almost weary.

She twisted in her seat until she could sit on her knees to face him. "Did you ever think that maybe Evan and Yelena could be friends to me? I'm going to need some of those when you're gone. Evan's nice to me." In a weird way that intrigued her when it shouldn't, sure, but she was only beginning to know them. "And he wants me to be friends with his sister."

"That's not–"

"I know! I know your thoughts. But it's not fair for you to leave me and make it hard for me to make friends without you."

Even in the last of the sun Kahrin could see him blink. "I–I didn't think about that."

"You're latched on to this idea of Yelena being a unicorn."

"She is. I know it."

"Fine. I at least believe that you believe that, and I'm working on the rest." Oh, that sounded so *mean*. "That was less judgy in my head."

He shrugged. "It's fine."

"It's not. I'm sorry." She unbuckled her belt and crawled over the seat to his lap and curled up. "We'll keep looking into it, just, please try not to piss off the people I have to be around when you're gone. Hm?"

"Hm?" he asked. "Did you just *hm* me?"

She shrugged. "I've listened to your sermons long enough, I figured I'd give it a try." Which resulted in fingers in her ribs and hips, and Pretty Mouth's pretty mouth growling into the join of her neck and shoulder. She squealed, squirming, batting at his hands until she wrestled him into abandoning it. Of course, it took some quick thinking and quicker kisses, but she got there in the end.

"Fight over?" she asked, a lift of hope at the end of the word.

"I can think of better things to do with our time." Now it was his turn to shrug. "Where were we before we were rudely interrupted?"

Kahrin butted her forehead to his before she scrambled over the seat to the back. "I think I remember. Hurry up, and I'll freshen your memory."

CHAPTER SEVEN

Kahrin

"You're sure you don't need me to pick you up, then?" Da asked her the next afternoon. He pulled the truck up to the curb in front of the Greveses' house, and the diesel engine settled into a rough purr. A grim line tightened his lips as his eyes settled on the old-style house.

Kahrin rolled her eyes with affection. She didn't want to say she was the stereotypical Daddy's Little Girl, but she knew it applied, at least in part. "Yes, Da. Innes will pick me up when he's finished tutoring." Nerd.

Da quietly nodded his head. "You'll come straight home?"

"Where are we going to go on a school night?" She chuckled, this little dance she and Da did amusing her more than anything. He pretended to question Innes' intentions, she pretended to take it seriously.

"There's a lot of empty road between here and the house." Da gave her one of those sidelong looks that said more than his words ever could. The tattoos leftover from his youth with his tribe sometimes made him imposing, especially to those who did not know his still and quiet nature, or the impulsive romantic who left home to marry a woman his family did not like. That was the point of the tattoos, simply put. Something about having ink tamped onto your head and neck with an awl and thread had that effect on people. Her only objection was Da's objection to her interest in having them done herself. "Just be careful."

"We're always careful," she said pointedly, full well knowing they were no longer speaking of driving. "Innes would never hurt me."

"Do you think he'd make it past the door of my house if I thought otherwise?" The corner of her mouth twitched as she acknowledged his point. Their door had never been closed to Innes ever since Ma's interrogation of him upon his first visit. "The shared appetites of the young are not my only concern."

Kahrin laughed. "You know you don't have to be so protective."

"And yet I always am." Da nodded toward the house and inhaled like he was steeling himself. "Don't want to be late."

"Yes, Da." She pushed the truck door open, sliding off the seat to the ground with the hot-dish carrier handles slung over her forearm. "I love you."

"Love you, too, *makoons*."

Little bear. She'd not been 'little bear' in a very long time. Her cheeks reddened, forcing her to duck her head as she threw the door shut and headed up the path.

While it was pleasant, Kahrin was surprised Evan had invited her back to their home. She decided not to question it in the name of science. Or something. Her opinion of Evan was still up in the air, which was counter to Kahrin's tendency to make snap judgments on character. Naturally, she was asked not to bring Innes with her, hence the need for the evening pick-up. Usually that would be a deal-breaker, but a characteristic stubbornness made her dig her heels in despite knowing that made it a less safe situation.

She rang the bell, the old dirgelike tones giving her an eerie feeling that wasn't helping her opinion. It was a few moments before she heard the sound of footsteps approaching and she stood tall, the carrier now clutched in both hands.

"Kahrin," Evan greeted her, his voice low and tired but the smile he gave her warm all the same. That would have been all well and good, but something about Evan still made her uneasy. Innes called it predatory. Given the difference in age between them, Kahrin preferred *intriguingly inappropriate*. "What do we have here?" he asked, inclining his head at the quilted carrier.

"Pie. Apple." Ma couldn't understand how anyone could dislike Innes, so she did what she often did when faced with a problem she couldn't understand or fix. "It's a little cliche for a farmer's wife to make an apple pie as a gift, but hers is really good. She even makes the crust from scratch." Kahrin didn't know anyone else's mothers who regularly made pies, let alone the crust, so it seemed like a big deal to mention it.

He lifted an eyebrow as he stepped aside to admit her. "That was very generous."

"She feeds people. That's what she does." Especially when she was nosy about them, which was a nearly constant state for her. Kahrin set the dish down to remove her boots and parka.

"Well, I suppose we're people, are we?"

She didn't catch herself quite in time to hide the quizzical expression that scrunched her face. That was an odd thing to say. If Innes had been here, that being why it was probably good that he was not, he would have latched right onto that as proof of his theory about the Greveses. "Aren't we all?"

She hopped up off the bench and carried the pie through the dining room toward where she remembered the kitchen to be. As she crossed the dining room, her eyes fell upon Yelena, staring out the large bay window, leaning against the glass, partially obscured by the window sheer. The low winter sun highlighted the blues and purples of her pale skin, adding an odd, ethereal quality to her. She didn't look up when Kahrin cleared her throat.

Stopping her trip to the kitchen, Kahrin set the pie on the dining table, half afraid the worn quilting would sully the elegant runner that stretched down the center. Kahrin made a promise to try and understand Innes' concerns, and that meant she had to make an effort to get to know the mysterious girl. "Hi."

Yelena glanced in her direction, a dim smile that didn't quite reach her large, glass-blue eyes. "It's good to see you again." She sighed, her gaze drifting out the window once more. "Mister Cameron is not with you."

"Nope." Kahrin shifted her weight from one foot to the other, as if Yelena's stillness meant she had to compensate with extra fidgeting. "He said to say 'hi.'" He hadn't, but only because she'd not thought to ask him. She was sure he would have if he'd known Kahrin would be quizzed on it.

"Oh." She didn't move, didn't look to Kahrin again. She just stared out the window, looking sad in a way that made Kahrin's chest hurt. She wasn't just sad. She looked devastated, but in the most calm way possible.

So, this wasn't awkward at all.

Kahrin gnawed at her lip, rocking on her stockinged

feet. She had to think of something, or this was going to be a long night. Kahrin could barely endure this quiet, let alone an entire evening. "Do you like slasher movies?"

"Hm?" That got her attention. She turned to meet Kahrin's eyes. "What do you mean?"

A tilt leaned Kahrin's head. "You know, slasher movies. People getting killed by weirdos with knives and stuff. Most of them are ridiculous if you remember they're fake, but they also have a neat pattern if you watch enough of them, so it can be fun."

Yelena shook her head. "Sorry."

No, Kahrin figured as much. "There's this dumb thing we do, me and Innes. We build a blanket fort in the living room and eat too much red licorice and sour gummies and stay up all night watching them. See who can get the other with the most jump scares. Maybe next time you could, I dunno, join us?"

"At your farm?" There was a lift in her tone at the end. It was the most emotion she'd heard when Yelena wasn't screaming her head off. Kahrin nodded. "I–" Yelena's mouth clamped shut, her eyes trained just over Kahrin's shoulder. Kahrin turned to follow her gaze.

"Yelena doesn't do well away from the house for long periods," Evan explained as an interruption. He paused in the arched entryway to the dining room, pulling on a pair of supple leather gloves.

"Perhaps they could bring their sour gummies and movies here?" There was that little lift again. Hope, maybe?

"That boy only upsets you."

Yelena's beautiful face screwed up. "I like him."

Evan's face pinched, his confusion mirroring his sister's. "I'm sorry. No."

Well, that sucked. Kahrin lifted and dropped her shoulders to let Yelena know she tried. That wasn't her only idea, just the only one she was willing to argue right now.

"I will only be a few hours," Evan explained, motioning for Kahrin to follow him, his fancy shoes shifting tone as his steps went from hard floor to rug and hard floor again. "Help yourself to anything here, but please, no guests, and do not leave. I am afraid she may hurt herself if left alone. Or you, in your condition, if you both leave."

A sinking feeling in her stomach made the smile of agreement she gave him a little off. He didn't seem to notice, or if he did, he chose not to mention it. "Where are we gonna go?" she joked. "I don't drive, and it's too cold for walking." That's when his face darkened, just a little, his sallow features pulling into a frown that made her have to consciously not step backward. "We're gonna stay right here until you get back," she assured him.

"See that you do." His voice gave her an actual chill as he opened the door and stepped outside.

Kahrin breathed a sigh of relief. Opinion shifting. No matter what she'd said to Innes about needing to make friends, she wasn't sure that Evan Greves was someone she wanted to be one of those friends. She mistrusted him. Sort of. Not as much as Innes did, but that was the point. It made him interesting. She wanted to decide who she did and did not trust. He wasn't going to be here next year; she was.

"He doesn't let me out of the house."

Kahrin jumped, a shriek escaping her throat. She turned about quickly to find Yelena very close. Maybe a step away. She'd not even heard the floor creak as she stepped up behind her. "Cough or something, okay? Or put a bell around your neck." She tried to laugh it off as she swallowed her heart back to her chest where it belonged. Kahrin took a large step back, and stepped around her with exaggerated motions. "A little protective, then? I can relate."

"No. He doesn't let me leave, ever." Her voice stayed even, that breathy quality evident, even as she was clearly distressed. "For any reason. That's why you're here, to make sure I don't." Yelena's eyes narrowed as she stared at Kahrin, stone still. "I could leave with you."

"Do you like pie?" Kahrin thumbed over her shoulder toward the dining room once more. "Best apple pie you've ever had. I swear." She backed up a few steps, motioning for Yelena to follow her. If she put something in her mouth she couldn't say weird things. It worked for Innes, when he wanted Kahrin to quit talking.

"I don't think I've ever had it." She followed Kahrin, the crestfallen expression she wore too much for her to bear.

"You're going to love it. It's practically criminal that you've never had it." She reached for Yelena's hand to urge her to follow.

Yelena jerked back, her eyes going very wide and wild. "Don't!"

Kahrin lifted her hands to both sides of her head. "Sorry. I won't."

This was why she didn't have friends who weren't Innes. She knew Innes and could predict his reactions before she did something. Usually. Okay, sometimes she was wrong. But other people weren't that easy. She slowed her pace to Yelena's, waiting for her to take a seat before she slid the pie plate out of the carrier. Forks retrieved, Kahrin pushed the plate between them and offered one to

Yelena.

Yelena's clear eyes scrunched as she slowly took a forkful. They ate in silence for a few minutes, Kahrin shifting in her chair back and forth on the tufted seat, making the wood squeak. "So. How's your memory? Anything coming back to you?"

Her entire focus on the pie, Yelena shook her head. "Not really, no. Glimpses. Something I can almost reach." She looked up to Kahrin. "I know you don't believe me," she said quietly. "You're very closed-minded." There was a pause as Yelena judged her words. "But your friend does."

O-kay then. Kahrin nodded, tucking an errant strand of hair behind her ear. "Best friend." Why she felt the need to clarify that, she didn't know. "And, yeah, he does."

"Evan's not my brother. I don't have brothers. He's not what he seems."

"I do. Trust me, you're not missing out." Yelena simply blinked, no other part of her moving. Even though Kahrin knew she was going to regret asking, she did anyway. "What do you mean, he's not what he seems?"

"It doesn't matter if you don't believe me." She took a small bite of the pie and put her fork down. "It's very good, just like you said." She was very still for a moment. So still, that if Kahrin hadn't been talking to her, she might have mistaken her for dead. Or one of those really pretty China dolls some girls had but weren't allowed to play with. Stupid, really, having a doll you couldn't play with. "Do you always mean what you say?"

Kahrin's brow creased. What kind of question was that? "Doesn't make sense to say things you don't mean. Just sends you barreling towards misunderstanding."

"Do you trust your best friend?"

Another weird question. "Of course. With my life."

She shook her head, her breath hitching as she fought tears. Oh, man, Kahrin couldn't handle tears today. "What about mine?"

"That's not fair."

"None of this is fair. Evan has me trapped here, and for some reason his magic, my magic–"

"Magic?" Kahrin dropped her head against the high back of the chair.

"It doesn't work on you."

Her head snapped back up, leaving a dizzy trail of stars in her vision. "What?"

"I'm trapped here. I can't leave. Except when you're standing at the door."

Kahrin blinked. "What?" Boy that word was starting to not sound like a word.

"The barrier parts for you. And Evan can't touch me, but you . . .," she grabbed Kahrin's hand, the same chill that whipped through her at the hospital running through her now as Yelena wound their fingers together, "you can. The magic doesn't work on you. That's why I couldn't heal you. That's why I couldn't protect you."

Kahrin pulled away, her expression sharpening. "What do you want? What barrier?"

"Call Innes. Call your best friend, whom you trust with your life. Let him believe for both of you. The two of you can get me out of here. Please. I think he's going to try to kill me."

Innes

"So, can you get me her number or what?"

Innes looked up from his class notes, ignoring the vibrating of his phone in his pocket as he painstakingly rewrote them. "I don't think that has anything to do with *Hamlet*," he pointed out to Carbry.

"Well, I don't want his number." Carbry lifted both brows, indicating this should be obvious.

Innes let a soft chuckle through his nose. "Yeah, given what happens to Ophelia, I don't think I'd want his number either." Was it a dodge? Yes. Carbry was getting off topic, and Innes wasn't being paid to play matchmaker with his best friend.

"Who?"

His phone vibrated in his pocket again. "You read the play, right?" His question was more stern than he'd intended. Thankfully, he got paid hourly and not based on results.

Carbry turned both of his palms upward and affected the best insulted look he was likely capable of. "Yeah. Of course I did. I just don't remember all the names."

He deserved a medal for not rolling his eyes. "Oh, well, that's simple. There's not a lot of women in *Hamlet*, so just remember she's the one that kills him at the end."

The look of confusion that clouded Carbry's features was not promising. Not in the way it should have been. He flipped a section of the script forward and began scanning the last pages. "Wait, he dies? So, who becomes king of Denmark?"

The third time his phone vibrated it came in a rhythmic series, which meant whoever was trying to get ahold of him (Kahrin) was growing impatient. "Ophelia. Obviously," he huffed as he stood from the chair, then took a calming breath. "Why don't you review the final act while I take this?" He lifted his phone, the nearly inappropriate selfie Kahrin had taken and assigned to herself in his contacts on the screen. Was it possible for a ring to sound exasperated? If it was, it would be Kahrin who could do it.

"Yeah. Sure." Carbry leaned his chair on the back legs and did as Innes suggested.

He was two steps out the door of the study room when he remembered where Kahrin was. The Greveses' residence. His steps doubled in speed for the library door that led to a small, interior courtyard.

"Okay, things are just weird, and I need you," Kahrin said before he could even say hello.

"Calm-" No, that wasn't going to work. "What's weird? Take a breath, count to three, explain what-"

"Screw you and screw your counting! I need you in your car and here, now." Her voice rose in pitch, though it sounded like she was trying to keep quiet. That did not make him feel any better. "This is your fault, you know. You got her all worked up and now she's talking nonsense and flipping out. I know Evan said you can't be here but-"

"Kahrin," he tried as she rattled on. Usually, if he just let her wind her way through her tangle of spinning thoughts, she'd get to the point on her own, but the panic in her voice knotted his gut, and he found he couldn't wait for her to get a grip on herself. "Kahrin," he repeated. "Kahrin, shut up." He heard her sharp intake of breath, but it worked. "Who's flipping out? Yelena? What did you do?"

"What makes you think I did anything?" she snapped. Innes knew that if they'd been in arm's reach of one another she might have slugged him in the arm. "Please, just get over here. She's yapping about someone trying to kill her–"

Wait, what? "Is Evan there?"

"No." Her voice cracked but she tried to cover it up by rushing on. "But I have no idea when he'll be ba–"

"I'll be right there," he interrupted. "Don't leave."

"Yeah, where am I going to go with a crazy unicorn girl and no car?"

With a sigh, he hung up and jogged back inside. "Hey, sorry, I have to cut it short today. Something's come up."

"Ophelia didn't kill Hamlet, man, she's already dead," Carbry said, words heavy with accusation.

"Worked that out, hm?" He neatly packed his books into his knapsack, feigning calm despite his heart beating against his ribs, and slung it. "Read the rest of the play and I'll see you in class." With loping strides he left the study room once more.

"Hey, you never answered my question, Cameron!"

"No," Innes called over his shoulder. It wasn't his place to tell Kahrin who she could and could not date, and sure, she and Carbry had a lot of things in common, but for Kahrin that wasn't really a good thing. He didn't have to make her inevitable boredom easy. Carbry could get her number himself if he really wanted it.

Thankfully, the roads in the city were dry and clear, making Innes' speeding less dangerous. In theory. He slowed enough at stops to make sure there were no police before he rolled through them, but in the end, he couldn't say for sure that any of it got him to the Greveses' house any faster. He did the drive-around, slowing enough to check for signs that Evan was home before circling the block and parking down the street enough to hopefully be out of notice. Just in case.

"Where the hell have you been?" Kahrin demanded as she threw the front door open. The rising panic in her voice was replaced with barely concealed terror. Her big, pretty, mismatched eyes widened further. Whatever was happening really had her worked up, which meant if he didn't calm her, she'd pull everyone else into her spiral.

"Instead of yelling at me for science's failure to perfect teleportation," he started as calmly as he could, "why don't you tell me what's going on?" He could hear crying inside. A sound that came like a blow to the head for how terrible it left him feeling, the sobs being thrust from the earth itself in a horrifying birth of grief incarnate into the world.

"Just come in," she said, moving away from the entryway and back toward the dining area. The smell of spices and apples reminded his stomach of how hungry he was. He would know the smell of Ma Quirke's pies anywhere, he was sure of it.

"No!" Yelena screamed. She came running in from the other room. "Don't come in. Not yet!"

Innes froze at the doorway, his brows lifted in alarm. "Then, what–"

"Look," she insisted. She lifted a hand, flat and palm-out, against the plane of the space of the doorway. Innes stepped back, instinctively, fearful that she'd accidentally touch him and sully herself with it. She pressed forward all the same, her hand flattening like she was pushing against plate glass. Iridescent ripples wavered outward from where she touched. Her clear eyes looked up to meet his, the intensity causing his breath to leave his lungs. "See?"

He did see. That didn't answer what it was that he was seeing. He lifted his own hand, attempting to cross the plane, only to see the same effect. An affirmation of what he'd known all along, and yet unlike anything he'd ever imagined. "Kahrin!" he called. When she didn't answer, he repeated it, louder, worry lacing his words.

"He's trapped me," Yelena continued. "I can't leave, and no one can come in without his permission."

Innes blinked. "Evan?" He knew it. He knew something was off about that guy, and it was all he could do not to whoop. Yelena nodded confirmation. "Magic?" She nodded once more.

Magic. Actual, real, honest-to-goodness magic. Any other time, he might have marveled at it, but they didn't have time for him to gloat right now.

"Okay," Kahrin grumbled as she came back toward the door, the pie carrier in her hand. Evidently the threat of wrath from losing Ma Quirke's cookware overrode panic at the moment, or it was the small details keeping Kahrin from losing her mind. "Great, so everyone here not currently brain damaged can see what's going on, I guess." She caught his gaze as it fell on the quilted carrier. "I don't know what's going on, but if he's really evil like you all say, he's not keeping Ma's pie." So straightforward, as if it should have been obvious to both of them. "I don't care how hot he is. She makes the crust herself."

That wasn't what really caught his attention, though. The closer she got to the door, the thinner the shimmering barrier became. It rippled, and started to peel back from the middle toward the edges, like when they'd dip their hands in glue in primary school to pull it off in strips and sheets after it dried. "How are you doing that?"

"How am I doing what?" she snapped. "I keep telling you," she looked to Yelena, "both of you, I don't know what you think is happening but I don't see anything." She strode through the door, easy as anything, widening Innes' eyes as she did so. As soon as she passed through, the iridescent shield snapped back together, swirls of chromatic swirls warbling in the wake. Kahrin gave no indication she noticed it at all. She didn't see it, and it had no effect on her. He touched it once more, just to make sure he'd not imagined it.

Yelena beat upon it with her fists. "Please, don't leave me here!"

Kahrin grunted her frustration, turning around on the ball of her foot and stomping back. "Fine." She stuck her hand through the door and grasped Yelena by the arm, starting back for the street once more before she'd even turned around. The barrier parted, letting both girls out before it snapped closed once more. The very end of one of Yelena's waves of blonde hair caught in it, snipping off neatly. When it fluttered to the floor on the other side of the barrier, it lay there no longer wavy and blonde, but shiny and white and smooth.

"Get in the car," Innes ordered, his timbre dropping low, but not for fun this time. They needed to leave. Now. "Hurry. We have to get out of here."

Kahrin threw her hands up in the air, her breathing erratic the way it was before she broke into crying. Whatever had her agitated, she was on the edge of crumbling from it, and he pulled her against him with one arm tight around her for just a moment, kissing the crown of her head. "I feel crazy," she muttered against his chest. "Everyone's seeing and hearing things, except me, and expecting me to know what to do."

"It's okay." How did he sound so sure? He had no idea what was going on, beyond the fact that he saw magic, and he saw his best friend dissolve it. He saw proof of his suspicions. He felt unshakable in his beliefs. Was that what it felt like, being a hero? No, this was no time to get caught up in boyish fantasies, even if it seemed he was actually living one. "I've got you."

He jerked his chin at the car, far down the street, and released Kahrin. "Where are we going?"

"Anywhere but here," Kahrin called over her shoulder. As she gained Yelena's side, she wrapped her unencumbered arm around her, and urged her to hurry. Yelena didn't pull away, or shriek. "Not the farm. I don't want him near my family."

Great. That didn't leave a lot of options, but they all loaded up in his little K-car anyway, and he started driving out of town. As if they were being chased.

CHAPTER EIGHT

Kahrin

Kahrin pressed her temple to the cool window, letting the rhythm of the tires on the road soothe her breathing. Three bumps in, three bumps out. She didn't like to admit when things scared her, but this did. All of it. Things she couldn't see or hear or feel, happening all around her. If she said she saw it, too, she was a liar, but when you didn't see things other people did, it made you sound a little crazy. There was nothing wrong with being crazy, but questioning reality around you didn't feel good.

Yelena sat in the middle of the back seat—even though sliding to one side would have given her more room—with the console in the middle and Kahrin's knapsack taking up the floor behind her own seat. When Kahrin looked into the sideview mirror to see Yelena, she was staring straight ahead, not unlike a spooked deer. When she looked toward Innes, gripping the steering wheel so tight his knuckles whitened, she could feel the tension rolling off of him like heat.

"Where are we going?" Kahrin asked, just to break the quiet.

"I don't know," Innes said. Sharply. She flinched. "So far you've only told me where we can't go."

Kahrin slid down in her seat and nodded. "Sorry." She

drew her knees up and put her feet on the dash, trying to make herself smaller.

"Kahrin." She could see the little muscle in his cheek flutter in irritation.

She dropped her feet down before tucking them under herself. "Sorry," she repeated.

He glanced at her. "I didn't mean to snap. I just don't have a plan. We had a plan. I did tutoring, then I pick you up, and we were going to go to the farm and watch a movie. We were probably going to," he dropped his voice and nodded his head toward her, "you know."

She let a huff. "Fool around?" Tension stretched so taut that she found herself unable to even muster up the spunk to tease him for struggling to say 'fool around.'

His cheeks reddened instantly, to the grey in his hairline and the brown of his brows. "Kahrin."

"I'm sorry I ruined your night." Yelena's voice carried like the flutter of butterfly wings from the backseat. Kahrin winced. Disappointing her physically hurt.

"It's not your fault," Innes said to her in the rearview mirror. Just in case he thought Kahrin would disagree, he looked at her. "It's not her fault."

"I know." Kahrin folded her arms inside her parka, sticking out her lip. Had she said it was Yelena's fault? No. If anything, it was stupid Evan's stupid fault. As if on cue, her phone started to buzz and she pulled it from her pocket to glance at it. "Crap. It's Evan."

"Don't answer!" Yelena shrieked. She lunged forward and swung at Kahrin's phone. "He knows we left! He can't find us."

Kahrin dodged her swing, holding it out of her reach. "If I don't answer, he's going to keep calling."

"Turn your phone off." Innes leaned his hip toward her. "Mine, too. If it's not on, I don't think you can track it."

That sounded like solid logic. She hard-powered hers down and reached into Innes' back pocket to do the same to his.

"Is that back ten behind your field still empty?" Innes asked.

Kahrin looked at him, confused. "Back ten?" What did that mean?

"Doesn't your family rotate fields? The back field is empty this year, right?"

"It's winter, Innes. They're all empty," she told him slowly.

"Right." Why was his jaw still so tight? Wasn't that a good thing? She closed her eyes, trying to get a handle on her spinning thoughts and the vertigo making her nauseated.

"Seth Fisher's dad has a shelter in his south cow pasture." It was as good a place as any. "The cows stay in the north field in winter because that barn's heated."

"Sounds good." Finally! The car engine hummed louder as Innes accelerated with a destination in mind.

"No." *Wait, what?* She heard Yelena scramble across the seat, pressing against the passenger-side window. "There. Stop there!"

"We're almost to the farm," Innes insisted, glancing into the rearview again. "Don't worry. We'll park in the barn, out of sight of the road."

"No, I remember being there!" She slapped her hands on the window. "Please. There's something there. I need to go look." She thrashed around the back seat, wild and determined. "I have to."

Kahrin twisted around in her seat. "It's not far up the road. You'll be safe there until we–" She would have kept going had Yelena not pushed the car door open, the sudden vacuum it created drawing their hair across their faces. "Yelena!"

She dropped from the car, rolling into the bank of snow. Kahrin's seatbelt snapped tight as Innes' foot slammed on the breaks. She bounced off the back of her seat as he swerved sharply to the side of the road, the underside of the car scraping on the rough snow.

"Is she okay?" he asked as he unclipped his belt.

Kahrin rubbed at her forehead, seeing stars and trying to shake it off. "I don't know." The words barely left her mouth when her stomach turned over violently.

"Are you okay?" he asked, focusing on her for the moment. His brow furrowed, the concern familiar and obvious. "Kahrin?"

"I'm fine." She was clearly not fine, rubbing at her eyes and clutching her head, but she needed to give him permission to check on Yelena. Kahrin understood the importance in this, and resigned herself to it. "Go make sure she didn't break her neck."

He leaned across the seat and lightly kissed her temple. "I'll be right back. Stay here."

He looked to make sure no cars had come up on them before he swung his legs around and climbed out of the car. He was already mid-stride by the time his feet hit the ground. Kahrin leaned against her seat, closing her eyes. She let out a deep breath. Unicorn or not—and she was still decidedly in the 'not' camp—Kahrin was going to wrap her hands around Yelena's pretty throat if she just caused Kahrin a second impact concussion. She breathed in, then out, and tried to relax until they came back.

If she drifted off, she didn't know. She knew she wasn't supposed to, but with no one around and her head feeling like it did, it was hard to do otherwise. Clearly she had not died, and instead woke up to a shrill scream cutting through the quiet.

"Kahrin!" The pitch of Innes' voice made her heart stop, and she shoved the car door open, being jerked back by her seatbelt. She belatedly remembered to undo the buckle, then tumbled out the door onto her hands and knees in the snow. She vomited. Ma's pie tasted way better the first time, she thought in her stupor, and she breathed out hard as she blinked tears from her eyes. Innes yelled again. "Kahrin! Run!"

Kahrin looked up, sure she was seeing things. A black van had parked a few hundred feet behind them. Two men had Innes by the arms, shoving him in, and Yelena was, what? Lassoed? That made no sense. Unless Innes was right. She couldn't deal with that thought right now. They were all in danger. Kahrin staggered up from the ground and immediately fell against the side of the car, her fingers scraping for purchase where there was none to be had. "No," she barely managed. "Innes, no."

The van spun about in the street, the tires squealing as it started back the way they'd come. Kahrin slid down, her back against the car, and let out a sob. There was no way she could catch them, even in the car. She wasn't that good at driving yet, and she could hardly see straight, besides.

Kahrin fumbled to pull her phone from her pocket, powering it on. The screen was scarcely loaded when the phone buzzed, and Kahrin blinked several times at it. Evan Greves. Even in her daze, she knew this was no coincidence. "I can explain," she started before letting him say anything.

"You don't need to," Evan assured her on the other end, his voice oddly honeyed. "My sister can be very convincing. However, I can't trust you on your own anymore, Kahrin."

"No. No, that's not true I can . . . I can . . ."

"I have something you want, and you have something I want. So," she looked up to see a black sedan pull up behind the car, "if you want your friend back, you will get in the car."

She let a hard sob and looked up at the dimming sky as a tall man in black approached her, dragging her from the ground without ceremony.

Innes

Once he was sure Kahrin was okay, and no car was going to run him over, Innes was out of the car and running back toward where they'd lost Yelena. He found the place where she'd rolled out of the car and followed the trail of her footprints through the snow past the tree line.

"Yelena," he called, pitching his voice low so it would carry. He slowed to a halting pace as the snow grew deeper, coming nearly to his knees with each step. His strides required him to almost march as he navigated through the birches and pines, following what he hoped was her tracks.

Had Evan been right? Was she just a very sick girl? If they'd brought her out here, only to get her lost, hurt, or worse, was this his fault for not listening to Kahrin? What if those same boyish fantasies had just put an ill young woman in danger?

His longer legs eventually gave him the advantage when he saw a flash of her parka between the trees as she fell over, letting out a high cry. "Yelena," he called again. "Please stop."

She clambered up out of the snow, her pretty face flushed from exertion. "I remember this place, Innes." Trudging a few more steps, she used the trunk of a tree to get her balance. "It's the last thing I remember."

Innes paused in his stride, some of his momentary doubts easing. "What do you remember?" He held his hands up in placation as he moved closer. "Tell me. Maybe I can help piece it together."

"I was here. I remember being here, scared. I was . . . I was running." She spun around, her clear-blue eyes wide and wild. Her gaze landed on him again, and she stepped back to keep space between them. She stumbled in the snow and fell onto her rear. "Someone was chasing me." Her hands lifted up in warning.

He returned the gesture. "I won't touch you," he promised. "I just want to help. Remember? Kahrin wants to help. We're going to help you. We'll go back to the car, together, okay?" He had no idea what helping her was going to look like. Their plan had been half formed at best. What would they do next? Live in Old Man Fisher's barn forever?

"You believe me?" she asked.

"I do." He nodded to reaffirm it, feeling the wet cold as the snow covering jeans started to melt. "What else do you remember?"

Her head whipped around in a swirl of loose, bobbing, blonde curls, hearing something he could not, her breath coming out in puffs of fog. He could no longer tell the terror on her face from the usual startled-looking way about her. Innes followed her line of sight, seeing nothing out of the ordinary. Trees. Ever-lengthening shadows.

She didn't move back this time as he stepped forward. He reached his hand out to offer her help up, jerking it back suddenly to avoid spooking her further. He had promised, after all. The muscles of her throat moved as she swallowed. "There were men, chasing me. I think–I think they worked for Evan, but I–I don't remember." She trailed off once more, then met his eyes. It made his heart beat harder, that protective rush rising in him once more. She stared at him, as if seeing through him, or reading his very thoughts. The winter breeze through the trees tossing a single wavy lock of hair across her face. "You know what I am."

Innes' brows lifted, surprised, even though he'd expected the question for quite a while now. Something in her face asked before she ever spoke the words. He gave the only answer he could possibly give. "I do."

How was it possible for her to look relieved and tense at once? She was a series of contradictions, like Kahrin, but in wildly different ways. He knew that it was the situation spooking her. She contradicted herself because she was a contradiction. Not a human at all, trapped in the body of a human. Her voice was high, thin, the words showing her as desperate for something she couldn't quite reach. "What am I? Say it. Please. I need to hear it."

"You're a unicorn."

He said it. Unicorn. He formed the word with his own lips and said it out loud. Somehow it didn't sound silly, like he thought it might. That just proved that he'd been right.

Knowing dawned in her eyes, as if his words had let all

the missing pieces fall into place. A small smile lit her pretty, round face, that sadness from her clear eyes lifting for the first time since they'd met her. He couldn't help the way it brought a smile to his own face to see hers light up. A peek of sun through grey clouds.

"Thank you, Innes." She stood a little taller once regaining her feet. Steady. "I remember. I remember everything. I remember those men of Evan's chasing me." Her eyes darted here and there around them as she looked for things he could not see or hear.

"Why?" he asked without thinking. "Why does he want you?" According to all the various stories, there were any number of reasons someone could want a unicorn. But why did Evan Greves want it?

"My heart."

Innes' eyes widened. "He wants to kill you." Well, that was the only way to get her heart, wasn't it? Protectiveness surged in him once more, making blood thunder in his ears. "We have to go." He gestured back in the direction of the car. Once they got in the car, they could drive farther past the farms. There had to be a way to turn her back. They could go to the city if they had to.

"His magic requires life force. It drains him to cast even simple spells." She reached for his hand to steady her as they started walking back toward the road, but he pulled away. He couldn't let her touch him. Especially not now that he knew he was right. This time it was her who looked surprised.

"And your heart is an infinite life force." Because she would be immortal in her natural form.

Their breathing became labored as they approached the road. "Yes. But magic protects me. He can't touch me or hurt me, especially now that he's changed me. It took all his strength to keep me trapped in that house."

"Wait." Innes stopped, his brown eyes narrowing quizzically as he tried to put the pieces together. "How was he going to get your heart if he can't hurt you?"

Her large, nearly colorless eyes met his, as if passing the thought from her mind to his. And maybe she was. She'd done it before. She'd been in his mind, asking for his help. Now it was just one word, an image really, and one that made his heart stand still.

"Kahrin." He picked up his pace, torn between staying at Yelena's side and getting back to his best friend. His injured best friend.

Yelena screamed. A shriek so harsh it could have shattered glass. Rope lassoed around her, jerking her back toward a man in thick gloves and a black peacoat. "Run!" she screamed to him, and though it pained him, he did. Without hesitation.

"Kahrin!" he yelled as he broke the tree line. He skidded to a stop, a large, black van blocking his path. He tried to dart around it, his sodden boots sliding in the wet snow. "Kahrin, run!" he called again as two more men got out of the van. They were on him so fast he hardly stood a chance, the first wrenching his arms behind his back as the other dropped a black bag over his head. Were they kidding? Kidnapping, and they couldn't leave him the dignity of unruffled hair? Someone grabbed his legs, no matter how he kicked and twisted, and then lugged him along by his now-bound limbs. With a heave, they tossed him unceremoniously into the van.

Behind him he heard Yelena shrieking, and then a sound that could only have been the men tossing her in beside him. He felt her back press against him, making him go rigid in horror, but as she started sobbing into the floor of the van, he couldn't bring himself to pull away. They lurched to one side as the van turned about quickly.

CHAPTER NINE

Kahrin

Her head hurt. So much. She couldn't let Evan know how desperately she wanted to lie back and close her eyes and just drift off. It just seemed too much like giving him an upper hand to admit she wasn't fully herself. Letting the arguably creepy man who may or may not have been flirting with her in an inappropriate way she may or may not have appreciated know that her brain was a little off right now did not sound like a solid survival tactic. Watching the road made her dizzy, and watching the trees blur past made her nauseated, which left Kahrin with the window visor to focus on. That made it difficult to ignore Evan, who hummed softly with some Berlioz dirge-sounding classical crap that sort of creeped her out in a *Sleeping with the Enemy* way.

"I underestimated you, Kahrin." She glanced at him, the yellow pallor of his skin off-putting even in the evening light. Had she really found him attractive not so long ago? Ew. That did not help her nausea. "You were too closed-minded to believe their stories." He made a quiet tsk. "I couldn't believe my luck when I discovered what you are at the hospital."

She turned to look at him, her face pulled in disgust. "What I am?" She pinched the bridge of her nose, trying to focus on the pain to keep her thoughts in the present. "What I am is freaked out because some weird man has some possibly gross fixation with me babysitting his not-sister." She sat back in her seat, slouching down and crossing her arms over her chest.

A smarmy smile turned up his lips. Even in the dark she could see the dark hollows of his eyes. He was weak. Wherever he'd been, if he'd really been getting treatments for anemia, they were not working. Somehow, like everything else going on, Kahrin didn't think he was being honest about that. Oh! A shock! The Bad Guy had lied to her. She lacked a medical degree, but probably it wasn't anemia making him ill. "How did you work it out?"

"Work what out?"

"The truth about Yelena."

Kahrin blinked. This seemed like one of those situations where only giving information specifically asked for was a good strategy. "What about Yelena? That she's not your sister?" She shrugged. "Just a hunch."

He laughed. Not that usual reserved chuckle she was familiar with, but an almost cruel sound of amusement. He was definitely making fun of her. Whatever it was he thought she was, it made her ignorant in his opinion. He shook his head, pitying her. "You really don't know, do you?"

"I don't know a lot of things. You'll have to be more specific." She looked at the door. If Yelena could leap from the car, she could, too, right? It wasn't exactly Plan A, but it was a plan. One of her hands slowly reached for her seatbelt.

Evan grabbed her hand before she could reach the buckle. "I wouldn't do that if I were you." He gestured to the door with a jerk of his chin. "Your friend will not thank you for it."

Her lips pressed into a hard line, her fatigue, nausea, and pain forgotten as her voice dropped into a warning tone. "What did you do to Innes?"

"Nothing, and if you cooperate with me, it will stay that way."

"I'll kill you," she promised.

"I highly doubt that. I might not be able to read your mind, but unfortunately for me, I know you are not a murderer." Evan let out a weary breath. "You are special, Kahrin, though it's likely you've never known it."

She scoffed. "Okay." She rolled her eyes, immediately wishing she hadn't, and leaning her head against the window, welcoming the cold of the glass. "I'm special. Great. So that's why I'm going to be stuck here in this stupid town until I die of boredom."

"Do you know how rare magic is, Kahrin?" He slowed, turning onto a dark road, which was considerably less clear of snow than the one they'd been on.

"Not you, too." She groaned. "If it's so rare, then why is it all anyone can talk about right now?" She threw her hand up. "There's no such thing as magic."

"Perhaps not to you."

"What?" She turned toward him again. "What does that mean? Like, I don't believe in it so I can't possibly understand it?" No streetlights. Clouds covering the moon. The only light available was the promise of the town not far ahead of them and Evan's high beams. She did not like this. Her only comfort was that she was sure he was not planning to try to get lucky. That ship had sped away, full steam ahead.

"Magic exists all around us. It touches every part of life. There are only a handful of us in the world who can manipulate it. Once we were many, but magical bloodlines thinned and eventually died out, and knowledge was lost." Did he know what he sounded like? "Most people will never know what it is to bend the world to their will."

"What? Like a wizard?" If he donned a hat and robe, she really would jump from the car.

Evan sneered. "No one uses that word." He glanced at her. "At least no one with a shred of self-respect. I am an Adept."

Calling it a fancy word didn't make it less ridiculous. She snorted. "You're digging deep into supervillain tropes, I see. Monologuing. Batty stories." Innes had read her enough fantasy stories for her to recognize it. She flapped her hand like a puppet. "Bending the world to your will? Prove it."

He laughed again. "I would if I could, dear girl. The effort and life force would be wasted on you, I'm afraid."

Her jaw tensed. "Figures."

"Adepts manipulate magic. Most of the rest of the world cannot. Even if they believe in it. They can see it, feel it, and be affected by it, but not use it." He slowed as they passed through a flurry that required he adjust his steering. "Then, there are a precious few out there for whom it does not exist." His eyes flicked to her, then back to the road. "Like you."

"That sounds like the same thing twice." They were going around the town now, which she'd only noticed when they didn't cross the small bridge over the creek.

"It does not exist to you, and you do not exist to it. Were magic a sense, it could not know you. You, Kahrin, are something most adepts fear: a hole in the world. The opposite of magic."

She barked a laugh. "Right. Okay. Now I know you're full of it." She twisted around in her seat to face him, drawing a leg up and under her. "And I supposed you're the bravest Adept who ever lived because you're not scared of my . . . hole-iness."

"Oh, I was, at first." He laughed at some private joke she would never hear. "As useful as you might be—and have no doubt as to your usefulness—if you figured out what you are, you could use it against me." That low, refined chuckle sounded from the back of his throat again.

"So, what makes you think I won't?" In answer, he drove the car through an unmanned gate and up a narrow gravel drive to a set of Quonset huts, arranged in two long rows, each with a floodlight hanging from the front. He brought it to a stop behind a dark conversion van, and Kahrin's heart skipped. "Innes," she whispered. Her brow furrowed as she craned her neck to look around the yard for any sign of him. Seeing nothing hopeful, she turned a glare on Evan. "What is it you want me to do?"

She expected thugs like the ones who'd dragged Innes and Yelena off to descend upon the car and drag her out of it. But nothing of the sort happened. They simply stopped. Evan turned the car off and unlocked the doors. He made no move to stop her. No indication that he'd try to interfere if she decided to run. Evan Greves was that certain, and rightfully so, that Innes was the perfect leverage over her.

He looked at her, eyes too dark to discern in the flickering floodlight of the nearest Quonset, but the smile on his face sent a shiver through her. His lips parted from teeth reflected in the harsh light.

"Say it," she snapped. "That's what you're waiting for, right? The big dramatic moment where you reveal your nefarious purpose, demanding I help you or you'll hurt my best friend?"

"You read too many stories," he chastised.

"Joke's on you," she spat back, "I don't read at all." Someone had to embrace how ridiculous this all was. Besides, she wasn't lying, exactly. Innes read to her, usually.

"You're going to kill Yelena, and bring me her heart."

She burst out laughing, shoving her fingers into her hair the grasp her aching head. "I knew you were going to say that." She held up a hand as if to stave off the absurdity of it all. "And yet, I was not ready to hear you actually say that." Cupping a hand over her mouth, she tried to get control of herself. This was far from funny, after all. He had Innes and Yelena somewhere and was willing to kill at least one, probably both of them. "If you're such a powerful wizard Adept person, what do you need me for? You can't take a heart out of one little teenage girl all on your own?"

Evan let out a long, resigned sigh. At least she had the advantage of annoying him. In the grand scheme of things, it did her no good, but she got to be smug about it, and she'd take what she could right now. "Because she's a unicorn," he said, because of course that's what he said. As if that explained everything.

Innes being right about all of this was exactly what this whole situation was missing. She wished he was sitting here with them, for many reasons, but not least of all to see his face at the vindication of his stubborn belief. If they lived through this she would never hear the end of it. She'd take it over his death, but still. She could already imagine his insufferable *I told you so* every time the topic came up again. And it would. Of that, she was certain.

"My magic is useless against her." That was interesting. "She's weaker as a human, her memories gone and magic unsteady. The spell to change her is quite draining." His eyes bored into hers, and that nauseated feeling spiked again. "Even her weak magic protects her from me, but not from you."

She shook her head. "No. No, I can't do that. I'm not going to kill her."

Whatever calm Evan had maintained all this time broke, her refusal a stone shattering the surface of the pool as he gripped her hand and growled through gritted teeth. "You will bring me the unicorn's heart, or I will bring you his."

Kahrin

If Kahrin had any delusions that she would be given time to think about the choice laid before her, she was quickly disabused of them. And abused, as it turned out. The door to the sedan was thrown open and she was wrenched from it.

"No, no, no!" she shrieked, arms and legs working to hold on to anything in her reach. "Wait. I just need . . ." What? What could she possibly need to consider in this situation? Neither option was even possible, as both required her to kill someone, one of whom was her *best friend*, which was not on her list of things to do today. "I need to think!" The man who had her under the arms, holding her in such a way that her legs only bicycled as she kicked them to get loose, grunted for her to shut up. The pain behind her eyes was blearing.

Evan stepped out of the driver's side of the car, leaning hard on his cane, and looking even more sallow in the floodlights. "You've had enough time to think." He nodded toward the heavy sliding door on the front of the Quonset. "Take her inside."

Between the sick feeling in her stomach and the pain in her head, she wouldn't have been able to think anyhow. Evan rapped his cane against the door, and after a series of loud clanking, it was hauled open from the inside. The man carrying her set her down and shoved her through the opening. She stumbled forward, falling to her hands and knees with a yelp of pain as she landed on the concrete.

"Kahrin?"

She looked up, the inside of the building dimly lit by the same sort of caged lights Da used in the barns. Even with her blurry vision she could see Innes and Yelena, tied to separate support beams in the center of the single room. A ring of dark powder had been poured around Yelena. Innes' hair stood in disarray, adding to his appearance of being worse for the wear. "Innes," she murmured back, mournfully.

Innes pulled at the restraints holding him, a snarling growl coming from deep in his throat. "Don't hurt her."

Evan let a low chuckle, his closed lips muffling the sound. "I have no intention of doing that." No doubt someone who would make a person kill a unicorn could find a dozen uses for someone with Kahrin's unique gifts. Or lack thereof. She wasn't sure. He jerked his chin in her direction. "Get her on her feet. She won't run."

He had her there.

The taller of Evan's thugs, the one who'd carried her in, walked over and grabbed her by one arm, hauling her to her feet. The room spun, forcing her to clench her eyes. Even as her thoughts scattered about, all staying just out of reach, she managed to shrug away from the man's grip. "It's going to be fine, Innes." She couldn't promise. It wasn't her place to do so, and she couldn't guarantee it, as much as she wanted to. Saying nothing felt worse.

Evan stepped forward, his long, gloved fingers wrapping around the head of his cane. He pulled it back, drawing out a blade of glossy, dark metal. He turned it handle first toward Kahrin. "You'll need this." It was heavy, two of her fingers wide and as long as her hand. It felt cool against her skin, but she noticed nothing else unusual about it. She looked up, meeting Innes' eyes, wide and more afraid than she'd ever seen him in the years of their lives together. Whatever he saw, she did not, adding strength to Evan's absurd story of her being a hole in the world or whatever.

"No," Yelena sobbed, the word drawn out to several more syllables than necessary. Or maybe it was exactly necessary, as she, too, seemed to recognize the blade in Kahrin's grip. "No, please." She bucked and pulled against her own restraints, though the ring of powder surrounding her kept her motions limited in range.

Evan gripped Kahrin's chin, forcing her to meet his eyes. His fingers pressed just behind the join of her jaw, lighting her whole world with a bright flash of pain. His eyes looked faded and hollow as he examined her face. "You are a very pretty girl, Kahrin. I actually regret that you're too dangerous to keep near me. That you've survived to this age is remarkable. Anyone else would have destroyed you on first introduction. Either your charms are more universally appealing than I believe them to be, or you're being protected."

She glared at him, her face twisted in disgust concealing her confusion at the utter nonsense dumping from his face hole. Behind her, Innes made a sound that wrenched her heart in her chest. "Gross," she spat at him. She jerked her face free and looked over her shoulder to Innes, then Yelena, grief gripping her guts. "If I do what you ask, you won't hurt him?"

"All I want is the unicorn's heart."

"What?" Innes yelled. "Kahrin, no! You can't do that."

She pulled her lip over her teeth and bit down, fighting back a shaky cry as she ignored Innes' plea. She kept her focus on Evan's eyes. "Promise."

"Would you believe it if I did?" He had a point, and she turned her head away, feeling defeated and helpless. "I thought not." With a gentle hand, Evan urged her to turn around to face her best friend, and the supposedly magical creature he'd thrown himself into danger to protect.

Yelena's sobs became something closer to a growl, her knees bending, the bindings supporting her now dropped weight. "Kahrin, you can't let him have my heart. He'll be unstoppable."

"Quiet," Evan snapped. He leaned over Kahrin's shoulder so his words were right in her ear, though he made no effort to keep them concealed from the others. "I need it cut from her chest while it still beats. If you kill her first, it's useless to me."

Tears slid from Kahrin's eyes as she heard Innes growl another threat that she knew he'd never be able to carry out. She shook her head back and forth, slowly. "I can't do it, Evan. Please. I can't cut out her *heart*." The thought made her gorge rise, and that was just at the idea of cutting open someone who was dead. But a screaming, crying, flailing person? There was no way.

Evan smiled beside her, his cheek pressed to hers. "If you don't, or if you fail, I will plunge that dagger through your best friend's chest while you watch. That blade is darksteel, and it will hold his soul." Kahrin flinched. "I will have the unicorn's heart if I have to kill everyone you care about to convince you to take it from her."

He gave her a weak shove, which in her state was enough to send her stumbling forward. Regaining her balance, she walked as steady as her dizziness would allow until she was in front of Innes.

"Kahrin, you can't do this," Innes pleaded with her. "Please. You can't hurt her."

"I don't want to." Her face contorted in misery. "I'm some kind of magical hole and her magic won't stop me. If I don't do it, no one else can." She looked up into those big, bistre eyes of his, scared that she'd never be able to again. She tipped up on her toes. "I love you, and I can't imagine the world without you in it."

"Kahrin stop." He shook his head, tears formed on his thick lashes even as he tried to pitch his voice sternly. "If you kill a unicorn, your life will be forfeit in the magical world."

She shook her head. He didn't know how wrong he was. Or, at least she thought so. If Evan told the truth, her life would be forfeit in the magical world anyhow. "Your hair looks like crap," she said as she reached up to fix it. He made a frustrated sound, which she ignored as she leaned up to claim a kiss. "I'm sorry I have to do this."

"You don't," he yelled now. "You have a choice, Kahrin. You can choose not to do it."

"I know." She turned so she didn't have to look at him anymore, not sure she would be able to stand the look on his face. With a deep breath, she strode slowly toward Yelena, whose clear eyes widened with the instincts of something feral. Not with fear, but something more akin to outrage. She stomped and pulled at the rope binding her. "Don't do this!" she told her. Not a plea. Yelena was not begging for her life. She spoke with all the haughtiness of a revered being. She expected to be obeyed. "You know what I am, and you know you shouldn't do this."

"I know," Kahrin said, stopping just outside the circle of what appeared to be iron shavings. She stepped over the ring, her hand placating as if soothing some animal or another. Her eyes never left Yelena's, mismatched hazel focused tightly on glass blue. "Trust me," she whispered.

"Do it now, Kahrin!" Evan called to her, as if afraid she'd forget he was there. As if she'd forget the sword hanging over her head on so thin a wire as her wavering courage. She wouldn't forget. She'd never forget what corner Evan Greves had backed her into. "Quit stalling."

Yelena's nostrils flared, but she held Kahrin's gaze with her chin high, a look of understanding hardening her impossibly beautiful features. Hands shaking, Kahrin lifted the dagger, Evan's voice, Innes' voice, everything but herself and Yelena falling away from her. With a quick motion, she cut the rope that held Yelena to the support post. "Protect Innes!" she growled, scuffing her feet backward and scattering the ring of iron wide enough for Yelena to pass through. Once outside the ring, before she could stop herself, she drove the dagger into her own abdomen, below her navel, a pained scream tearing from her throat.

Somewhere behind her, someone screamed out. In front of her, as she staggered, someone screamed. Yelena's foot slid in a splatter of Kahrin's blood, and iridescent light glimmered and rose around her. Her face elongated and she fell forward with a cry that turned into something more of a dreamy, far off whinny. As Kahrin let herself drop to the ground, just before she blacked out from the pain, she saw an honest to goodness unicorn.

"Innes was right," she mumbled.

CHAPTER TEN

Innes

If this entire day hadn't been barely managed chaos, Innes might have thought he hallucinated the events that had just taken place. They made no sense, or at least no more sense than anything else that happened today. In a terrifying realization, he knew that if he believed that one of the things he witnessed was real, he had to believe this, too. That fact slammed into his head like his car into a tree as he finally managed to comprehend that Kahrin had just driven a knife into her own belly.

His pulse pounded in his ears, drowning out the havoc that exploded in the room following her singularly stupid act. If his chest had caved inward, crushing his lungs, he wouldn't have been surprised. He screamed out her name, something he felt tear from his throat, but couldn't hear.

Somehow, the *unicorn* in the room was the only thing that made sense.

He pulled hard at the restraints, the ropes biting into and burning his skin, though he hardly felt it. He jerked hard, feeling the wooden pole shift even as the ropes held tight.

Everything came crashing back to him at once, too loud and too real, at the sight of her blood on her hands. "Kahrin!"

She lay on the concrete ground, curled around herself and gasping in pain. She gritted her teeth, even now trying to hold back her whimpers.

"You stupid girl," Evan growled.

Innes didn't look at him, or if he did, he didn't see him. His attention was elsewhere. He watched the men who had hauled them in as they advanced on Kahrin. Yelena, or who had moments ago been Yelena, danced about her on cloven, tufted hooves, blocking them from her. Where it had taken only the three of them to get the pair of them into the warehouse, they couldn't get close to her now, even fanned out as they were. She nickered at them, raising up on her rear legs and kicking the front out. Her eyes flashed fierce, the almost-colorless blue vibrant against her white face, her formerly wavy blonde hair tossing about in shiny white-blue locks.

Innes pulled again, harder this time, the ache in his chest bringing tears to his eyes. Or more tears. At some point he'd started crying, though he could not have pinpointed when. He pulled once more, his eyes bulging, and this time when it hurt he didn't give in to it, and yanked himself free.

Yelena kicked one of the advancing men in the head, and he collapsed to the ground. Innes was behind them in three strides.

"Enough!" Evan's voice boomed through the room and everything around them froze. Except Yelena, and Kahrin on the ground. Evan's hands were raised in front of him in the air. A streak of fresh, red blood dripped down the length of it, and an odd green glow tinted the air, creating a boundary between Evan and the rest of them. "I want her heart." Innes felt pressure on his throat, and he lifted from the ground ever so slightly. Just enough that when he kicked his feet, the toes of his shoes barely touched the concrete. Close enough to know relief was there, too far to attain it. "One of you will die if I do not get it!"

The henchmen were not spared Evan's wrath. Each of them, clad in all dark colors of snug-fitting clothes looked as alarmed as Innes felt. The neck of one snapped and fell to the ground, leaving only one, an unmistakable streak of wet forming at the bifurcation of his trousers. Yelena stomped back and forth, snorting in challenge as if daring Evan to advance on her. Or, more likely, it seemed, advance on Kahrin.

The harder it became to draw a breath, the harder it became for Innes to stay calm. Everything sounded tinny and far away. Until he heard Kahrin sit up with a pained groan. He willed her to stop. Who knew what damage she'd done to herself, or what more she'd do now? "Stop it," she rasped. She clutched at her gut, clearly straining. "You're angry with me."

Evan laughed, cold but weakly. Whatever he was doing was killing him, or near enough to it. "I am, and I told you what I would do." Innes felt the invisible coil squeeze tighter around his throat and chest. Much more and the pressure might snap something. The remaining thug's eyes began to go dim, and Innes' heart thrummed with the certainty that he was next. Yelena dashed up to the shimmering barrier, attempting to break through it, but it held her back. "Now, get up, Kahrin, and do what," Evan paused and gasped for a breath, and for just a moment, the pressure Innes felt lessened, "do what I told you."

Innes drew a rasped breath, quick and not quite full, but enough to refresh before Evan snapped his hand into a fist once more. He was weakening. The magic was funneling the energy out of him. Yelena retreated and charged the barrier once more, thrusting her front hooves against it and sending odd green sparks off in a halo around each one. The more she did this, the further Evan seemed to strain.

With a scant sound, Innes fought against the hold. He kicked his legs, toes of his shoes just scuffing the floor with barely a motion. His reward for his efforts was a tighter grip around his chest, and he felt the pop of what was surely a rib giving way. But this time, when Yelena attacked the barrier, it warped. The wall of it pushed inward, elastic and giving the more she leaned. It snapped back into place, sending her skittering back with another loud snort. As it did, the pressure loosened, and Innes was able to snatch another breath.

Help me fight. The breathy, whispery sound of Yelena's human voice echoed in his panicked mind. *Fight, Innes. I need you. He can't defend against us both; he's too weak.*

Evan couldn't hold both! Using the moment of distraction that was Yelena prancing in front of the barrier, looking for a way through, Innes strained once more, this time, raising his arms but a few inches from his sides. Kahrin grunted, on her knees now, wan and looking as if she might topple forward at any moment. He tried to yell to her, to beg her to stay down until they could get help. Even if he'd been able to force the words out, he had no guarantee she would listen. More likely she'd tell him she was fine and just needed to walk it off.

Evan advanced, pushing the barrier forward with him and forcing Yelena back, closer to Kahrin. The effort loosened his hold on Innes almost entirely, and he wriggled to the ground, gaining traction with the soles of his shoes and pressing forward almost two full steps towards Kahrin. Yelling out in pain, Evan snatched him in place once more, and Yelena was able to stretch into the barrier once again, her roar filling the entirety of the Quonset.

Pulse deafening in his ears again, Innes could feel himself turning purple. Another rib cracked, and though he fought with all he had left, he couldn't get loose again.

"I will crush him, right here in front of you," Evan muttered, the toll on him obvious. "Do it, Kahrin, do it now." Even if she'd wanted to, Innes had no idea how Kahrin would even take on Yelena, ferocious and enraged as she was, her long neck shaking her horned head from side to side.

One foot, and then the other, with a scream Innes would never forget, Kahrin managed to her feet. Yelena rounded on her, rearing up, but Kahrin stood her ground, her eyes steady. There was nothing Innes could do but watch. Yelena paced one way, and then the other before neighing. She stomped her hooves on the ground and neighed once more. It was a few quickened heartbeats before Innes realized the unicorn was communicating with Kahrin in the only way she could figure how. Kahrin couldn't hear the words she whispered into his mind, but this aggressive stomping and braying seemed to reach her.

Kahrin staggered, one step, and then another, one hand still around the hilt of the blade in her abdomen. Innes struggled against the hold again, and the closer she got to him, the easier it became.

"No!" Evan roared.

He turned all of his attention to Innes as Kahrin threw herself at him, free arm catching him around the back of the neck. They toppled to the ground, Kahrin shrieking out, and Innes gasping loudly, his lungs relishing the feeling of euphoria at being full once more. He cradled her to him and ducked his head. "You're so stupid," he cried against her neck.

When he looked up, Yelena was pressing through the barrier. With every step she took, Evan retreated, his eyes frantic as he desperately pulled at his spell, trying to fold the barrier around him, his blood spilling dangerously fast. Now Yelena galloped around him, herding him where she wanted him. She lowered her head, jabbing her long horn toward him. His sallow face pulled more and more gaunt, and this time, when Yelena reared up to dash her hooves on the barrier, it flickered and finally disappeared. She kicked out again, her legs cycling around like bike pedals, forcing him back again until he ran out of space and she struck him. First in the shoulder, then square in the chest. She hardly needed to do more, yet it did not stop her from goring him with her horn, so long that it looked impossible for her thin neck to even hold it up. His skin stretched in on itself, and Innes looked on in horror as he rapidly aged before him, thrashing and seizing as he curled up. The last sound he made, a rattling rasp, dissipated into the room, and then everything was silent.

Too silent. As if all the sound in the world had been sucked out with Evan Greves' life. Kahrin went limp in Innes' arms, and he trembled with an overwhelming rush of emotions; anger and grief and helpless fear all warred to be the first expressed.

Yelena was near them in the blink of an eye, time and space seeming to have no control on her whatsoever. And why should it? She was a unicorn. He'd been right this whole time. He only wished his heart didn't feel shattered so he might appreciate it more, or that Kahrin were still here so they could see her together.

Yelena lowered her head, and Innes shrank back, still afraid that somehow he'd dirty her. She was more beautiful than her human form could ever capture, the light refracting into rainbows across the coarse fur of her coat. She dipped her head once more, nuzzling just beneath Innes' jaw. The sensation from the single point of contact bloomed out, warm and cold at once and washing over him like a gentle tide. It left him with an eerie calm, nothing happening in the moment able to shake it. He stroked Kahrin's hair with a clarity of mind that reassured him enough to not give over to tears and panic.

Yelena stepped back away from the pair of them. Innes blinked, his eyes begging to stay closed, though he fought it. He didn't want to miss a moment of this. When he opened them once more, she was gone. This time, he didn't fight the urge, he couldn't, and curled protectively around Kahrin as he let the blackness take him. At least they were here, together, at the end.

Then he felt Kahrin's phone vibrate in her pocket.

Yelena

Yelena watched from across the barren field, tall reedy grass whistling in the winter air, the moonlight on the snow concealing her. The humans wouldn't see her, not the ones who weren't looking for her. They didn't know because they didn't want to. It mattered little to her either way. She existed, and had for so long, that they rarely concerned her. Until now.

She watched as the vehicles pulled up with their flashing lights, first the police, and then the ambulance. People raced into and out of the little sloping warehouse, caught up in their lives and feelings. They wore their emotions loudly, crying out and calling orders to one another. So noisy and so chaotic, the world of humans, which she'd remained ignorant of. Until now.

In all the many years she roamed the Earth in joyful solitude, going where she pleased and when she wished, she met so many creatures. Some knew her for what she was, and some did not see her at all. She had little opinion on the matter. They came and went, lived and died in the blink of an eye. She remembered them all, but not really. Flits and flashes but nothing significant. What could possibly be notable to a unicorn when it no longer existed in her periphery?

Evan Greves was not the first to seek her out. Many an Adept over many a year sought her heart for their own gains. A rare prize, the heart of a unicorn. None had gotten as close to succeeding as Evan. It had been a stroke of luck in his favor that he found a Hole in the World—that gap in magic that could undo it all by letting it crumble at the seams. A Hole in the World destroyed the protections of the fantastic simply by existing, parting the mist and obliterating glamours that kept them safely concealed. Most of them were drown at birth, or as close to it as they were discovered. This one had been very lucky. Someone had gone to great pains to conceal and protect her.

Yelena knew she'd been lucky as well, for the Hole in the World had been swayed by love, the most weakening of human emotions. Love of a True Believer, no less. How, she wondered, did a True Believer come to love a Hole in the World? The very antithesis of everything he held in his heart, everything that made him who he was, he kept closer than any other. Yelena did not fully understand the hot bolt of pain that sheared through her heart. Like something had suddenly gone missing. It was a terrible feeling, and not one she wished to feel anymore.

All of which added up to many reasons why she could never return. The Hole in the World could bring ruin to magic, even if the True Believer stayed at her side. Perhaps he would temper her. Perhaps the forces that protected her life thus far would keep her from causing irrevocable harm.

As for the True Believer himself? Despite the terrible feeling, the sacrifice of the Hole in the World swayed her to sympathy. His pain changed her, and she'd allowed herself to touch him, to offer the only peace and comfort she knew. Yelena didn't know what that meant, since it had never happened before, but who could be touched by a unicorn and not be forever marked? It would have to suffice. Just as well the Hole in the World was here, for he might have tempted Yelena to stay. To what end? To watch him whither and die and feel this sadness more keenly? No. Better to forget him now than long for the cut of the dagger later when she'd be weakened further.

Her eyes lingered until she saw the pair of them off, tucked quickly into the back of their emergency vehicles, with a violent blaring of sirens and a terrible flashing of harsh lights. Then, following the path of the light of the moon, she disappeared into the woods, a tickling breeze blowing away the cloven hoof prints trailing behind her, until the only trace of her presence remained on the line of the jaw of the True Believer.

CHAPTER ELEVEN

Kahrin

Before she let the world tear her eyes open, Kahrin snuggled into the warmth that cocooned her. For a few minutes she rested with her ear against the steady thud of a familiar heart and breathed in the comforting scent. It wasn't until the whir of machines and beeps of monitors drew her attention, out of place in her mind, that Kahrin finally allowed herself to be drawn to the world of the awake. She smiled helplessly to discover Innes' arms about her as they curled together in her hospital bed.

She stayed very still, not wanting to disturb him as she put pieces of memory together, unable to remember how she got from the warehouse to here. That, and the pain that assaulted her became unbearable, swaying her to do little to provoke it further. It was enough to feel his face pressed into the curve between her neck and shoulder, and to hear the reassuring sounds of his breathing. He smelled so good, like home, no matter where they were.

Eventually stillness became unsustainable, and she wiggled her toes, both to make sure she could, and to let off some of the energy of being too still for too long. Even that little motion caused him to stir, and he lifted his head, big, brown eyes bleary, and smiled that beautiful smile of his. "You should have woken me," he chided gently.

"You seemed peaceful," she murmured. Her throat cracked lightly, and she swallowed to try and wet it with little success. "If I know you, there has been little sleep in your schedule."

He smiled still, though his brows knitted. "Whatever gave you that idea? It's been two whole days."

"If I'd seen you stab yourself, no one would have moved me from your side, no matter how many days it was."

"That was stupid of you." He pressed a kiss to her temple all the same and gently disentangled himself to reach for a cup of ice chips. It was then she noticed the bandages around his wrists, and the way he cringed at the simple motion of reaching.

"Stop," she scolded him, frowning. "You're injured."

Innes laughed softly, very shallow, indicating there were more injuries than she could see. "Just a little bruising." He narrowed his eyes. "Do you want to start that conversation already?"

She shook her head against the pillow, her head reminding her that she was still injured. "I'm just relieved you're okay."

"I am, now that you're awake."

Kahrin closed her eyes for a moment, taking a deep breath before moving in an attempt to sit up. She whimpered sharply before Innes reached across her to press the button that would tilt the head of the bed for her. "How bad is it?" she asked as she tried to get comfortable at the new angle. The pain in her gut flared, causing a cramp in her shoulder she did not like, and she winced.

Offering her an ice chip, which she promptly accepted, Innes took a measured breath. The tightness of his expression answered her question, artificially. It was bad.

"You're very lucky. You had two surgeries. One to . . ." he trailed off, giving Kahrin reason to frown.

"What?"

"I should let your parents tell you."

"Just tell me, Pretty Mouth." There was a bit more bite to her words than she meant there to be, but in her defense she'd just been stabbed and had two surgeries. "You can't dangle that in front of me and change the subject."

He still hesitated, running a chip of ice over her lips to moisten them before letting her take it into her mouth. "They had to remove your uterus." He shrugged, frowning in the realization that there was nothing he could offer to soften that. "I'm sorry."

"Oh," she said, her eyes moving from his to the ceiling. "Okay."

"Okay?"

She rolled up one shoulder and dropped it. "I had to pick something, and I reasoned I could live without that."

Innes propped up on an elbow. "Wait, what?"

Stretching to loosen some stiffness in her neck, Kahrin turned her head. "All those stupid anatomy tests. If I aimed low, I knew I'd be likely to survive it. I don't need any of those parts." Innes lifted a brow. "Children aren't important to me. My best friend is. Besides, what if the weird thing that's wrong with me is like, passed on?"

"What do you mean? What's wrong with you?" He offered her another chip of ice, deciding she wasn't going to tear him a new one for coddling her. Honestly, if a girl couldn't take some coddling after stabbing herself to save some lives, what use was she?

She breathed in slowly, then let it out. "Evan called me a Hole in the World. It's why he wanted to get close to me."

"Because you repel magic." Someone had been doing his homework. Nerd.

She shook her head slowly. "Not repel. More like, make it not exist at all." She let a soft chuckle of disbelief, which took more energy than she reasoned was good. "It's weird, because it's something I can't even see or feel."

"Or hear."

"Or hear," she agreed, remembering how Innes heard Yelena's voice when she could not. "I didn't even believe in magic."

"Do you now?"

"Does it matter?"

Innes stayed quiet a moment. "You saw a unicorn. You helped save her life."

"True." She sighed. "I suppose that changes things."

"You suppose?"

"You're going to hold the unicorn thing over my head, aren't you?"

Innes' big, bistre eyes widened. "Um, I knew she was a unicorn. If our situation was reversed, you'd be insufferable." He nudged her cheek with his nose. "The least you can do after scaring me senseless and not believing me is letting me have this, hm?"

Kahrin rolled her eyes. "Oh, I get a *hm*, do I?"

"You're going to be getting quite a few of them." He frowned in disapproval. "Don't you ever do that again. I thought I lost you."

"I thought I was going to lose you."

"How about if next time you wait until you're a little surer?" His pretty mouth turned up in a crooked grin before he added another, "Hm?"

"Fine." She laughed, wincing as it pulled at her

abdominal muscles. "We'll say that self-mutilation is a last resort, then. Whatever."

"Whatever." He brushed a bit of her hair from her forehead.

"Where are my parents?" she asked quietly. "If you're here, they must not be."

"Your Ma went for coffee."

"And Da?"

Innes pulled his mouth to the side. "He said he had to go out for a little while." He shrugged again. "He said not to let you out of my sight until he's back. He didn't say as much, but I think he meant I was promising on the pain of my very painful death. Painfully."

"I told you he likes you." She pecked a kiss on the end of his nose.

"He's being nice because we're both hurt."

"He's being nice because he knows you protect me if he can't."

Which reminded her. "How are you?" She nodded to his bandages.

"They're satisfied that I didn't mean to hurt myself. Turns out I'm stronger than I thought when I'm scared." He lowered his voice. "I told them that Evan is the one who stabbed you."

She nodded, going quiet for a time. "I'm sorry, Innes."

He lifted a brow. "For what?"

"I was jealous. I am jealous. I don't know how to live my life without you." She rolled her eyes as he narrowed his. "Calm down. I mean, I've never had to, and I don't want to share you in the meantime. I want to be selfish with your time."

He pressed his forehead to hers, and they lay there,

sharing breath quietly. "I want to be selfish with yours, too. But, Kahrin, you won't be without me. Ever. We'll visit. You . . . you could come, too. After graduation." She knew that he knew she did not believe that, though he would never stop trying to convince her otherwise. Innes believed she was more than a pretty girl from a backwater, small-town farm. "I won't let you slip from my life."

She studied his face from this odd angle, his eyes melding together in her too-close vision, then nodded. "I know. Now." In an attempt to snuggle closer, she tugged at him. "Just don't leave me for a unicorn, okay?"

He laughed, touching the side of his face, her eyes following the path of his fingers. There was a small spot at the back of his jaw, visible as his stubble had grown in around it, but leaving the space the size of her thumb bare. The skin was slightly, but hardly noticeably, pink.

She clicked her tongue softly. "Even if she does give impressive hickeys."

He narrowed his eyes, gently rebuking her for being so crass about something she knew was very special. "Never." He gripped one of her hands, twining his fingers. "Now, rest. I think it's fair to say you owe me a movie choice, and we can't do that until you're well enough to go home."

She rolled her eyes once more, but her lips strained against another smile. "Whatever."

"I'll take that as agreement."

Innes closed his eyes, leaving them that way, as if it would convince her to follow his lead. Kahrin waited until his breathing began to even before she gave into it, and fell asleep letting her chest fall into rhythm with his.

ABOUT ATMOSPHERE PRESS

Atmosphere Press is an independent, full-service publisher for excellent books in all genres and for all audiences. Learn more about what we do at atmospherepress.com.

We encourage you to check out some of Atmosphere's latest releases, which are available at Amazon.com and via order from your local bookstore:

Heat in the Vegas Night, nonfiction by Jerry Reedy
Chimera in New Orleans, a novel by Lauren Savoie
The Neurosis of George Fairbanks, a novel by Jonathan Kumar
Blue Screen, a novel by Jim van de Erve
Evelio's Garden, nonfiction by Sandra Shaw Homer
Young Yogi and the Mind Monsters, an illustrated retelling of Patanjali by Sonja Radvila
Difficulty Swallowing, essays by Kym Cunningham
Come Kill Me!, short stories by Mackinley Greenlaw
The Unexpected Aneurysm of the Potato Blossom Queen, short stories by Garrett Socol
Gathered, a novel by Kurt Hansen
Interviews from the Last Days, sci-fi poetry by Christina Loraine
Unorthodoxy, a novel by Joshua A.H. Harris
the oneness of Reality, poetry by Brock Mehler

The Clockwork Witch, a novel by McKenzie P. Odom

The Hole in the World, a novel by Brandann Hill-Mann

Frank, a novel by Gina DeNicola

Drop Dead Red, poetry by Elizabeth Carmer

Aging Without Grace, poetry by Sandra Fox Murphy

A User Guide to the Unconscious Mind, nonfiction by Tatiana Lukyanova

To the Next Step: Your Guide from High School and College to The Real World, nonfiction by Kyle Grappone

The George Stories, a novel by Christopher Gould

No Home Like a Raft, poetry by Martin Jon Porter

Mere Being, poetry by Barry D. Amis

The Traveler, a young adult novel by Jennifer Deaver

Breathing New Life: Finding Happiness after Tragedy, nonfiction by Bunny Leach

Mandated Happiness, a novel by Clayton Tucker

The Third Door, a novel by Jim Williams

The Yoga of Strength, a novel by Andrew Marc Rowe

They are Almost Invisible, poetry by Elizabeth Carmer

Let the Little Birds Sing, a novel by Sandra Fox Murphy

Spots Before Stripes, a novel by Jonathan Kumar

Auroras over Acadia, poetry by Paul Liebow

Love Your Vibe: Using the Power of Sound to Take Command of Your Life, nonfiction by Matt Omo

Leaving the Ladder: An Ex-Corporate Girl's Guide from the Rat Race to Fulfilment, nonfiction by Lynda Bayada

Adrift, poems by Kristy Peloquin

Time Do Not Stop, poems by William Guest

Dear Old Dogs, a novella by Gwen Head

ABOUT THE AUTHOR

Brandann R. Hill-Mann is a Triple Bi (Biracial, Bisexual, Bipolar) speculative fiction author, playwright, podcaster, stage manager, and U.S. Navy Veteran from Sault Sainte Marie, Michigan. Brandann is part of the weekly Bi Bi Bi Podcast, and her short stories have appeared in various publications. She lives in Hawai'i with her family. *The Hole in the World* is her debut novel.